SPECIAL MESSAGE TO READERS

THE ULVERSCROFT FOUNDATION
(registered UK charity number 264873)
was established in 1972 to provide funds for
research, diagnosis and treatment of eye diseases.
Examples of major projects funded by
the Ulverscroft Foundation are:-

- The Children's Eye Unit at Moorfields Eye Hospital, London
- The Ulverscroft Children's Eye Unit at Great Ormond Street Hospital for Sick Children
- Funding research into eye diseases and treatment at the Department of Ophthalmology, University of Leicester
- The Ulverscroft Vision Research Group, Institute of Child Health
- Twin operating theatres at the Western Ophthalmic Hospital, London
- The Chair of Ophthalmology at the Royal Australian College of Ophthalmologists

You can help further the work of the Foundation
by making a donation or leaving a legacy.
Every contribution is gratefully received. If you
would like to help support the Foundation or
require further information, please contact:

THE ULVERSCROFT FOUNDATION
The Green, Bradgate Road, Anstey
Leicester LE7 7FU, England
Tel: (0116) 236 4325

website: www.foundation.ulverscroft.com

LEAVING LISA

At age seventeen, married with a three-month-old baby and suffering from post-natal depression, all Rosie could see was her life in a cage with a giant lock. Twenty-five years later, after having left her husband Jack and daughter Lisa, she runs her own business in Nashville. But while she's in England, she sees an engagement announcement in the newspaper — Lisa is getting married. And Rosie decides she wants to make contact after all these years, despite fearing their reaction. Will they find room in their hearts for her again?

ANGELA BRITNELL

LEAVING LISA

Complete and Unabridged

LINFORD
Leicester

First published in Great Britain in 2018

First Linford Edition
published 2019

A catalogue record for this book is available
from the British Library.

ISBN 978–1–4448–4225–8

Published by
F. A. Thorpe (Publishing)
Anstey, Leicestershire

Set by Words & Graphics Ltd.
Anstey, Leicestershire
Printed and bound in Great Britain by
T. J. International Ltd., Padstow, Cornwall

This book is printed on acid-free paper

Daddy's Girl

Rosie crushed the engagement announcement in her hands before quickly flattening out the newspaper cutting out on the kitchen table.

She felt her mother's eyes on her as she traced her finger over the face in the photo. After 25 years the features of Rosie's baby daughter were evident in the beautiful woman in the picture, smiling and gazing in adoration at a handsome, dark-haired man.

'Your auntie Viv sent it a couple of months ago. I wasn't sure . . . if I'd want to see it.' Maggie didn't mean to sound sharp. 'Sorry.'

Her mother's pain at losing touch with her granddaughter ran deep. Officially Rosie's parents moved from Cornwall to Watford to be closer to her father's family but in truth they couldn't take the slanting looks and whispered remarks in St Wenn any longer.

'I put it in an envelope all ready to send you in Nashville.' Heat bloomed in Rosie's mother's cheeks. 'Your father told me not to be daft so I changed my mind.'

'I suppose he called me a heartless . . . '

'Don't, Rosie. He's gone now.' Maggie wiped at her eyes. 'He worshipped you and never understood how you could leave.' Now Rosie wasn't sure, either, but at seventeen all she'd seen was a cage with a giant lock.

'You gave me money and got me a taxi to the station,' Rosie said quietly.

Her mother had always warned her against settling down with the first boy who caught her eye. Of course, Rosie didn't pay attention, any more than Maggie had when Vince Trethewey had flirted with her at a Christmas party and married her six months later.

Against her mother's advice, Rosie had married Jack then had Lisa, their own honeymoon baby.

'Only daughter of Jack Kitto,' Rosie read on the newspaper cutting. Bitterness rose in her throat. She knew she didn't deserve a mention but it still hurt to be written out of her daughter's life.

'You're going to Plymouth for your work so why not run on down to St Wenn?' Maggie suggested.

'And say what?' Rosie bristled. 'Hello, Lisa. Long time no see. I'm the mother who walked out when you were a baby. Congratulations on your engagement and by the way is there any chance of a wedding invitation?'

'Maybe it's time to make your peace with Jack,' Maggie persisted.

'Leave it be. They don't need me. They never needed me.' She'd told herself that over and over in a desperate effort to wipe out the guilt that never quite went away.

Rosie sensed her mother itching to say more and exhaled a quiet breath when Maggie turned away to fill up the

3

kettle. She suppressed a smile.

The last two weeks were the longest she'd spent in England since she moved to Nashville over 20 years ago and become a dyed-in-the-wool coffee drinker, but that made no difference. At regular intervals her mother still plonked down in front of her the same sweet, milky tea she used to love and ignored the fact Rosie tossed most of it down the sink after letting it go cold in the cup.

'Well, you can do what you like, love, but I plan to see our Lisa come out of the church on her wedding day.' A stubborn expression settled on her face. Most of the time Maggie was a quiet, accommodating sort of woman but when she dug her toes in nothing and no-one could shift her.

'You're serious, aren't you? How will you get there?'

'There are buses and trains.'

Yeah, and you use a walking stick and occasionally have dizzy spells. That's a great idea, Rosie thought.

'We don't have to talk to anyone — just wait outside the church and then leave.'

'We?'

'You've changed so much no-one will recognise you and as it's February we can wear coats and hats.'

'You're making it sound like a clandestine operation.' Despite herself, Rosie laughed. 'Fine. I'll be your chauffeur.' She wagged her finger. 'But I'm not going to the church — you'll do that on your own.'

Her mother's eyes gleamed and Rosie knew she'd been backed into a corner by a professional negotiator. Rosie suspected she'd regret her decision but there was no way out now.

*　*　*

'What do you think, Daddy?'

Jack Kitto blinked back tears as his beautiful, laughing daughter spun around in a froth of white satin and tulle. That's how he'd been ordered to describe the material in Lisa's wedding dress but to him, and he suspected most fathers on the planet, it was simply what turned their little girls into women. He forced a smile and struggled to regain his ability to speak.

'Don't you dare cry because you'll start me off,' she warned. 'Only a week to go.' Lisa wrapped her arms around him.

For a second, Jack could've sworn a drift of the unique scent of freshly bathed and powdered baby filled the air. If he dared say such a daft thing out loud she'd call him a right old saddo.

'I can hardly wait to see Gino tonight.'

This was their last few hours of being the two of them before the man who was almost worthy of his daughter would fly in from Rome this afternoon and head down to Cornwall on the next train.

'I really wish I'd gone to meet him at the airport.' Lisa sighed.

Jack didn't point out the dress fitting,

meeting with the florist and million and one other tasks they had ticked off the list today. It seemed that planning a wedding rivalled Hannibal crossing the Alps.

He smoothed his hand over her thick, shiny hair, inherited from her mother, along with her husky laugh and whip-smart brain. A fleeting pang of regret swept through him. Rosie should be here, fussing over their daughter and giving motherly advice.

Get real. Rosie's only advice would be to flee before making the big mistake of walking down the aisle — because that's what she confessed she wished she'd done six months after they were married.

'Earth to Daddy.' Lisa pulled back and waved a hand in front of his face. 'After I get changed can we pack a flask and take our pasties over to the park? We'll be warm enough if we wrap up.'

Jack couldn't refuse her anything today. His mum said it was a miracle she wasn't spoiled because he'd rarely said no to his only child. Luckily, her sweet disposition triumphed over his ineptitude and they had stumbled through her childhood and emerged the other side in a good place. He hadn't even been a proper adult when he rushed into marriage but grew up pretty fast when left alone with a three-month-old baby.

'Did you make an extra pasty for Gino?'

'Of course.' Jack's cooking skills wouldn't match to the wonderful food he'd tasted on holiday in Italy but, with money always tight, he'd been determined to learn how to cook during Lisa's childhood. He had spent hours poring over recipe books and experimenting until he got it right.

'Do you need any help getting out of all that stuff?'

'We'll never make a fashion lover out of you, will we?' Her deep grey eyes sparkled. 'This isn't 'stuff'. It's a Maggie Sottero tulle ball gown with dazzling Swarovski crystals accenting the bodice, a delicate satin belt and pearl buttons.' Lisa playfully recited the description that should be tattooed on Jack's brain by now, along with the string of numbers on his bank statement. Not that he regretted a single penny. 'Do you think Gino will like it?' A tiny frown crinkled her forehead.

You'll bring the poor man to his knees, Jack thought. He managed a nod before turning away.

'I'll see to our tea.'

'Love you, Daddy.'

He waved a hand in the air and kept walking.

Long Forgotten Memories

You've changed so much no-one will recognise you. Her mother nailed that. The chubby girl with her National Health glasses, bitten-off nails and cheap high-street clothes was so far in the rear view mirror Rosie could barely see her any more.

Years of working around the fashion industry along with a strict low-carb, high-protein diet, contact lenses, expertly dyed hair and weekly manicures meant she was comfortable with her reflection these days. And inside? Don't go there. Rosie smoothed down her figure-hugging grey dress and adjusted the pink and grey Dior scarf.

'Are you ready, Mum?' She knocked on the bedroom door and walked straight in, taken aback by the sight of

10

her mother slumped on the bed with red, puffy eyes as though she'd been crying for hours. 'What's wrong?'

'I've changed my mind,' Maggie said. 'We shouldn't go. You told me so in the first place and you were right.'

Rosie perched on the edge of the shiny blue quilt and clasped her hands together, silently begging her mother to pull herself together. When Rosie had abandoned Jack and Lisa the soft empathetic side of her shrivelled and died.

Nowadays she floundered when people asked too much of her emotionally which was ironic considering her career choice.

She had drifted into the wedding business after working for an estate agent who found locations for family celebrations and corporate meetings on the side. When she started Wedding Wishes, her wedding experience company, she chose the flamboyant, demonstrative Crispin for her partner to cope with the bride hand-holding part.

They'd worked together well for a decade, starting with a small office in Nashville before expanding to Charleston and Atlanta and were now dipping their toes into overseas destination venues.

'You know I've got to go to Plymouth anyway so let's get that far. After I'm done with my work we'll decide what to do next. We could simply meander on down to Cornwall and visit a few of the old haunts if you like.'

'I don't know, love.' Maggie plucked at a loose thread on her brown tweed skirt. Your aunt Betsy forgets to feed Waldo half the time and walks the poor thing to death.'

Rosie smiled inside. It wouldn't do their old overweight, lazy dog any harm for a few days.

'I know Dad was a home-body but you haven't left Watford in years and I suspect the change will do you good.'

'I suppose.'

'Wash your face and come on down. I'll take your bag out to the car.' Rosie grabbed the cheap red plastic holdall she remembered from long ago family holidays, crammed full then of buckets and spades for the beach and new flip-flops.

'You never used to be this bossy.'

Rosie ignored the rebuke and walked away, hesitating at the top of the stairs as a wave of uncertainty swept through her. Did she need her brain tested? Her mother just offered her an easy way out and she'd chosen not to take it. Returning to the place where her life fell apart was probably a bad idea.

'I'm sorry we weren't enough for you.' Jack's words on the day she left were etched into her heart. She should have contradicted him because it had been the other way around. 'I'll always love you and I hope you'll be happy,' he had added. Happy was an elusive sentiment she'd no time for.

Rosie took several deep calming breaths and reined herself back in. All she needed to do was wrap up the job in Plymouth, give her mother a few more days of her time and then fly back to Nashville and get on with her life.

★ ★ ★

The front door slammed hard enough to rattle the windows and Jack stopped work on his crossword. He glanced over the top of his reading glasses to spy Lisa's blonde ponytail swinging as she strode down the front path.

When his daughter hit her teenage years he used her ponytail as a useful mood signal. A certain carefree type of hair swinging indicated happiness but this was the 'don't mess with me' sort.

'Signor Jack, do you have a moment?' Gino stuck his head in around the door.

Jack had tried to get the young man to call him Jack but that was apparently too informal for his comfort so they'd settled on a compromise.

'Of course. Sit down.'

Gino stretched out on the sofa and every line of his body thrummed with agitation. He started to tap his right foot until Jack wanted to plead with Lisa's fiancé not to wear a hole in the carpet.

'I do not know how to ask this . . . '

'Then maybe you shouldn't.'

'I have to.' The words released on a heavy exhalation and he leaned forward, sprawling his palms over his bent knees. 'Do you know where Lisa's mother lives now?'

Jack recoiled.

'I'm sorry — I did not mean to upset you.'

Jack cleared his throat, fighting for a few seconds to get his act together.

'I'm not upset exactly . . . more surprised.' Over the years he had answered his daughter's questions as honestly as he could without hurting her, never wanting to leave the impression that Rosie's defection was Lisa's fault. Over the years, Lisa's interest waned and he couldn't remember the last time she mentioned her mother.

'I don't have a contact address but as far as I know she's living in America. I believe she moved to Nashville in Tennessee.'

Jack wasn't being completely truthful. By putting together snippets of village gossip and using basic internet search techniques he knew exactly what his ex-wife was doing and where she was doing it.

'As you say here, Lisa flew off the handle when I asked her about her mother.' Gino gestured out of the window. 'That's why I am sitting here and she is . . . '

'Not?' Jack's wry smile pulled a similar trace of humour from his future son-in-law. It baffled him that the young couple hadn't had this conversation until five days before the wedding. 'I'm sure Lisa has her reasons for not talking about Rosie so perhaps you should respect that.'

'For me I do not worry but my mama and papa are asking.'

Jack sympathised with the young man's distress and needed to find a way around the problem without going behind Lisa's back.

'What exactly did Lisa tell you?'

'Only that Mrs Kitto left when Lisa was a baby, you were divorced and she has never been back or even sent a birthday card or Christmas present.'

'That about sums it up. What more do your parents need to know?' Gino's gaze dropped away and it struck Jack that the Rossis were afraid Lisa might inherit her mother's flighty tendencies.

Anger snaked through him that they could malign his beautiful daughter but he struggled to be rational. The Rossis worshipped their three children and didn't want to see their youngest son Gino hurt.

Jack remembered asking Lisa a million and one questions when she phoned from Rome bubbling over with excitement about her new boyfriend. While working there on an internship for her London-based bank she'd been out several times with Gino, the newly promoted personnel director. As soon as she launched into a long description of the handsome italian it became glaringly obvious this wasn't another casual date.

'Lisa is not her mother. If you have any doubts, don't marry her. Rosie and I shouldn't have married so please don't repeat our mistake.'

'No. No. That is not what I meant.' Gino jerked upright. 'I love Lisa with every bone in my body.' He made helpless gestures in the air. 'My parents — they swaddle me.'

Despite himself, Jack laughed.

'I think you mean they coddle you. Wrap you up in cotton wool.'

'Why they wish to wrap me in wool?'

By the time Jack had stumbled through an attempt to explain the idiosyncrasies of the English language they were good again.

'I am going to find Lisa.' Gino sprang up and grasped Jack's shoulders. 'I am sorry I bothered you. I will make sure my parents do not ask any upsetting questions.'

'I suggest you start off by trying the park at the end of the road.'

'The park?'

'When Lisa was a little girl it was her favourite spot and she still goes there every time she's home to watch the ducks and the children on the playground.'

In Jack's mind he felt Lisa's small hand snuggled into his and saw his tiny pigtailed daughter in her bright red wellington boots and matching raincoat jumping in the puddles.

'We will be back later. Ciao.'

Jack sighed. Maybe he'd been wrong not to force more conversations with Lisa about her mother. Did she become silent on the topic of Rosie to avoid hurting his feelings?

Perhaps if he'd remarried things would have been different but the proverb 'Once bitten twice shy' was designed for him.

At seventeen he fell headlong in love with the bright, argumentative teenager with the challenging smoke-grey eyes and no woman he'd met since matched up to Rosie.

Not that he'd tried very hard beyond the odd sympathy date fixed up by well-meaning friends. Saying Rosie's name out loud again forced him to delve under the neat pile of stones he'd stacked over his memories.

'Don't be an ostrich, Jack,' she had said. 'If you can't admit our marriage is a mistake, I can. We should have enjoyed a few fun dates and then gone our separate ways but you got serious, used the L-word and flashed a pretty ring around. I'm not putting all the blame on you because I fell for it. I'm no good at the whole wife and mother bit — surely you see that?

Jack startled as the front door banged open back against the wall. If he had a pound for every time he told Lisa off for doing that he'd be a millionaire. Hopefully when she had to paint her own house she'd be more careful.

Emotion tightened his throat as the looming change in Jack's life struck him

20

like a stabbing blow to the heart. Watching Lisa go off to university at eighteen was one thing and he coped fine when she was offered a job in London.

Even the six-month placement in Rome meant the opportunity for an Italian holiday. Lisa always made him proud and he'd never try to stop her following her dreams but a tiny part of Jack would disappear with her.

Lisa ran into the living room laughing and dragging Gino along behind her.

'Come on, Daddy, get your coat on and join us for a drink at the Red Lion.'

His immediate instinct to turn down her offer disappeared when he caught Gino's tiny frown. For the moment he'd push his concerns aside and concentrate on making his girl happy but at some point he must stop being a coward and bring the past back out into the open.

Never Too Late

Rosie was pretty sure the sign on the Tamar Bridge welcoming people to Cornwall didn't apply to her. She glanced across to her silent mother huddled in the seat. Maggie seemed to shrink further into herself with every mile they distanced themselves from Watford.

In Plymouth she'd appeared awed by Rosie's competent work persona, the one perfected over the years until little resemblance to her insecure teenage self remained.

The uncertainty started when the staff at their five-star boutique hotel on the Barbican made a huge fuss on their arrival. Her mother couldn't wrap her head around the idea that an endorsement by Wedding Wishes meant a huge coup for any business.

'So where do you want to go first?'

Over breakfast, Rosie tried to draw her mother out but that only set off another round of doubts ending with a plea to turn around and head straight back to London. At that point Rosie put her foot down. If Maggie wanted to see Lisa on her wedding day Rosie would move heaven and earth to achieve that goal. For a woman who fulfilled people's wildest wedding fantasies for a living this should be a piece of cake.

After all, if they were talking about cakes she'd found designers who could design one in every possible shape from a groom's childhood pet to a bouquet of freesias so lifelike a waiter attempted to water them.

'What about Penzance? That was your dad's favourite and you loved the swimming pool on the promenade. I saw in the paper they've done it up.'

She could warn her mother that in February the large seaside town wouldn't be the sunny, sub-tropical paradise of Maggie's memory but kept that to herself.

'Sure, we can do that. Penzance it is.' Her forced brightness sounded unnatural and judging by her mother's sidelong glance Maggie thought so, too. 'If the weather clears maybe we'll get the chance to check out Land's End and St Ives as well.' Anything to keep them away from St Wenn until the last possible moment.

'Auntie Vera's asked us over for dinner on Friday and your cousins in Padstow said to make sure and come by. If we've got time I told your Uncle Pete we might . . . '

'Who else have you blabbed to that we're coming?' Rosie checked her mirrors and pulled off to stop by the side of the road. 'This wasn't part of the deal.' She clenched the steering wheel to steady her shaking hands.

'But . . . '

'But nothing, Mum. At no time did I agree to visit any relatives or old friends. I can't . . . ' Her voice cracked and Rosie panicked that she might cry for the first time in 20-odd years. At the last second she won the battle and swallowed them back down. 'Sorry,' she muttered.

'No, I'm sorry. I'll ring and say we're too busy.'

'I understand, love.'

No, you really don't, Rosie thought — and if I explain I'll fall apart. She should have left straight after her father's funeral and returned to Nashville but she'd let her mother down enough and this way offered a chance for at least something in the way of payback.

'Let's press on and find somewhere to stay tonight.' She'd tracked down several possibilities online but staying at another fancy hotel would make things worse. 'I'm thinking a cute little B&B would make a change. Didn't we stay with a Mrs Hosking just off the seafront in Penzance?'

Her mother's astonishment lightened Rosie's mood.

'Fancy you remembering. She was a right old so-and-so. Banished us straight after breakfast until five o'clock in the afternoon and threw a wobbly if we tracked a grain of sand back in.' She chuckled. 'You spat out the tinned grapefruit and complained about the lumpy bed. Proper little fuss-pot you were.'

'Maybe it's best we don't try to track her down.' Rosie broke out laughing and her mum joined in. 'Come on, let's get going.'

★　★　★

'What's wrong, love?' Jack held out a slice of bubbling cheese on toast but Lisa screwed up her nose as if he'd offered her poison. 'Your dress fits perfectly — you don't need to starve for the next four days.'

'It's not that. I'm not hungry.' Her nervous edginess returned and she sprang up from the table to pace around the kitchen.

'Is everything OK with Gino?' Last night Jack had sensed a tension between the two but put that down to pre-wedding nerves.

'Yes.' The hesitant reply didn't reassure him. 'His parents are being a bit . . . iffy.'

Jack could either ask what she meant or be honest.

'About your mum?'

'I don't have a mother.' Lisa whirled around and glared. 'That's their problem. They're being all Italian. Family is everything to them and . . . ' Tears snaked down her cheeks.

Jack wrapped his arms around her and rubbed soothing circles up and down her spine. It always worked when she was a little girl and upset about something monumental like his latest inept effort at fixing her hair or being excluded from the 'in' group of girls in class.

'Every family is different and you're everything to me.' Jack brushed away a strand of honey blonde hair and an unsought memory of stroking Rosie's hair the day she had discovered she was expecting Lisa jolted him.

'A baby? We're children ourselves,' she'd wailed. 'What are we going to do with a baby?'

Jack had struggled to reassure his young bride while inwardly suppressing his own panic.

The realisation now that he wasn't enough for Lisa struck Jack like a freight train. He shoved his hurt back down and put on a brave face.

'On Saturday you and Gino will start a new family together and everything will change. That's the way it should be.'

'Gino's so close to his family he doesn't really get why I've no interest in my mother.'

For the first time ever Jack caught a hint of hollowness in her assertion.

'Are you sure that's true?' Her grey eyes flared with surprise. 'It's natural to be curious. You won't hurt me.' Jack grasped her hands. 'The wedding's brought all this on, hasn't it?'

Lisa stared down at the floor.

28

'I suppose so but it's too late.'

'It's never too late, sweetheart. Why don't you talk to Gino and see what he thinks? We could try to get in touch with her.'

'You're the best, Daddy.' She flung her arms around his neck. 'You're the least selfish man I know. Gino's got a lot to live up to.' Lisa snatched the toast from his abandoned plate and took a massive bite before running off with a smile on her face.

You've done it now, Jack told himself. He considered his options. He could contact Rosie direct or stand back and let Lisa do it her way.

Five minutes later he sat on his bed with the door closed and logged on to his laptop. With a wry smile he tapped in Rosie's name.

The familiar information he'd read over and over again flashed up the screen.

'Ms Rosalind Trethewey. Co-owner of Wedding Wishes, the premier wedding experience company in the southern United States.'

The glossy promotional picture made his ex-wife barely recognisable. She'd coloured her hair and restyled it. She had lost weight, highlighting cheek-bones previously blurred under the soft round features he recalled so well. Rosie's sharp black suit, white silk shirt and leg-lengthening black stilettos all drew subtle attention to her new sleek physique.

Jack managed to track down an email contact address but then struggled to compose a suitable message. After several frustrating minutes he hit Send on what he'd come up with.

Lisa would rightly be mad if she discovered he'd gone behind her back but he'd take that chance. He considered telling Gino what he'd done but that would put his future son-in-law in an awkward position. With any luck Rosie wouldn't respond and Lisa would let the subject drop.

He slammed the laptop shut and refused to consider what he saw as the worst outcome — which was his ex-wife returning to Cornwall. For his own peace of mind Jack never wanted to see Rosie again as long as he lived.

Family Matters

The rain wasn't letting up any time soon judging by the rivers gushing down the café windows. Penzance seafront was apparently out there somewhere. Rosie would force down another cup of coffee if that's what it took stay dry.

'At last.' Her mobile signal strengthened enough to start accessing her emails. The trouble with choosing an old-fashioned B&B was that the internet connection resembled using two tin cans and a piece of string.

For dinner last night they abandoned the idea of braving the non-stop rain and settled for steak pies and chips courtesy of their landlady. It was the first serious carbohydrates to pass Rosie's lips in years and tasted even better than she recalled.

'Do you want to see to your work

while I go for a wander?' Maggie offered.

The instant stab of guilt made Rosie set the phone back down on the table.

'No, I'll check them all later. Crispin's dealing with things from the Nashville end and he'll let me know if there's anything earth-shattering.'

'I think the rain's easing off a bit.'

Wishful thinking, Rosie thought.

'How about I run over to get the car and pick you up outside? If we head over to the other coast it might improve.' Cornish weather was unpredictable and might be different a few miles away. 'We could find a nice pub for lunch.' At this rate she'd be the size of a mansion by the time she got back to Nashville.

'That would be lovely.'

Rosie pushed her chair back.

'I'll brave it and discover if my new gear really is waterproof.'

'Blooming well should be, considering what you paid for them.'

Rosie had foolishly taken her mother

along when she went shopping but the casual way Rosie spent more in five minutes than Maggie would in about five years highlighted the deep divide between them.

When Rosie had fled St Wenn and headed for London she never intended to stay away from Cornwall for good. The knee-jerk reaction to being seventeen and trapped with no possibility of escape meant Rosie hadn't gone any further in her mind than getting off the train in Paddington and finding a bed for the night. Anything to get away from Jack's soulful pleading and her baby's incessant tears.

Rosie startled as her mother's cold fingers brushed over her hand.

'What's the matter, love?'

'What do you mean?' Her father always believed everything she said — until the day she walked out on her baby daughter. That was beyond his comprehension and their closeness never recovered from that.

But her mother could always cut

through Rosie's attempts to cover up her true feelings and at forty-three nothing had changed.

'I was thinking, that's all.'

Maggie's raised eyebrows said it all.

'I'm off.' Rosie headed towards the door. 'Be on the lookout for me in about five minutes because I won't be able to stop long.' She fumbled with her coat buttons and yanked the hood up over her head before the gusty wind whipped the door out of her hands. Rosie managed to step outside and then slammed the door shut behind her. Her return ticket to Nashville next Tuesday looked more inviting by the minute.

★　★　★

'You're a hopeless liar, Daddy.' Lisa giggled and grabbed Gino by the arm. 'You're no better, Gino — and I'm glad.' Her eyes shone. 'It means I'll always have the upper hand. Tell me right now what you were talking about.'

Jack tapped the side of his nose.

'Brides shouldn't ask too many questions a few days before the wedding. Let us men keep some secrets.'

'Fine. Be like that.' She gave a mock pout and brushed off Gino's attempt at a kiss. 'Some of us have work to do. I'll be back in about an hour.' Lisa waggled her unpolished nails around. 'The manicurist needs me to select my colour for Saturday.' She breezed out of the room and a minute or so later Jack heard the front door's familiar slam.

'I do not like to keep secrets from my beautiful girl.' Gino grimaced. 'I wish I had never mentioned about my parents fussing because I'm really not sure it is a good idea to stir everything up right before the wedding.'

'Sorry — but it's a bit late for that.' When Jack had confessed to sending the email Gino had winced.

'So what do we do now?' Gino asked.

'Tell her the truth before she winkles it out of us?' Jack suggested.

'Rosie . . . Rosalind or whatever she

calls herself now — she has not replied to your message. I think she is not interested. If Lisa gets the same result when she approaches her that will be that.'

'What happens if one of us gets a reply?' Jack asked.

'We deal with it then. Do not waste time now worrying.'

He envied Gino's optimism.

'If that's your wish I'll go along with it.' Jack determined to prepare for the alternative because he knew his stubborn daughter too well to believe she'd let this go.

★   ★   ★

Tramping around soggy Padstow in the middle of winter wasn't Rosie's idea of fun. In half an hour they were due at her cousin Pam's house for tea after being dragooned into it by her persuasive mother.

'I can't believe you and Pam lost touch. You two were like two peas in a pod growing up,' her mother had said.

After leaving Cornwall Rosie had ignored her cousin's phone calls and torn up her letters until they stopped coming because they reminded of everything she'd lost.

Pam's mother, Viv, was Maggie's younger sister and in the summer of 1970 they both married local men before giving birth to their first babies only weeks apart. When Rosie suspected she might be expecting, Pam was the first person she confided in but her cousin never forgave her for sneaking away and their lifelong friendship never recovered.

'It'll be good to see them again.' Maggie's smile dimmed. 'I know they all came up to Watford for the funeral but we didn't get the chance for a good natter.'

Rosie had avoided anything beyond exchanging sympathetic pleasantries on that awful afternoon, very aware if she once dared to let down her guard it would be impossible to get through the day.

Having intercepted enough curious glances then it wasn't hard to guess she was in for a major interrogation over the scones and saffron cake today.

'Let's go back to the car and head over to Pam's.'

'Remember they're family.'

How could I forget, Rosie felt like saying.

'I've been thinking I might get a passport,' Maggie suddenly said.

'What for?'

'Oh, I don't know,' Maggie laughed, 'maybe to visit my daughter in America?' Rosie stopped walking.

'Are you serious?' She rushed to soften the blunt question. 'Wow — that'd be lovely. You surprised me, that's all.'

'I'm sure I did.' Her mother's dry response made them both smile.

'Springtime is pretty in Nashville. It's usually warm without being too hot and all the blossoms will be on the trees.'

Years ago Rosie had tentatively suggested they visit but her father shot the idea down without giving his wife a chance to protest.

By unspoken agreement they didn't talk while Rosie drove the 16 or so miles to her cousin's house on the outskirts of Bodmin.

'There's Viv.' Her mother waved out of the window as they stopped outside. Before they went in, Rosie surveyed the bungalow, built of local stone and surrounded by a neatly trimmed lawn and flower-beds that even now held sunny daffodils and a few early pansies.

She compared this to her glossy, expensive high-rise condo in the centre of Nashville. If anyone called it 'homely' she'd be offended because the American definition of the word implied plain and ordinary but Pam's house was homely in the comforting sense.

Rosie stared at the sunny yellow front door and swallowed back tears as Pam appeared, unsmiling with her arms folded across her chest. If her mother believed that a cup of tea and a scone would make up for 25 years of neglect she couldn't be more wrong.

Asking for Trouble

Lisa frowned at the screen.

'She looks nothing like your wedding pictures.'

'No.'

'No? Is that all you've got to say?'

'What would you like me to say?' Jack ran a hand through his hair.

'How did she get from here to there?'

He bit back the instant flippant reply springing to his lips. Using humour to deflect his daughter wouldn't work.

'There must've been gossip going around St Wenn?' Lisa persisted.

'There were rumours,' Jack admitted. 'I know her parents left shortly after she did and an aunt moved over towards Bodmin way, I think. We lost touch.' Another guilt trip. He should've reached out to Rosie's mother and father but they hadn't contacted him, either, so he'd let it go.

'Don't stop there.'

Jack sighed and pulled out a couple of kitchen chairs.

'Sit down.'

'Will that make it easier?'

The brief version of Rosie's leaving that he used when Lisa was little satisfied her then but by the time she was a teenager she couldn't bear to hear Rosie's name mentioned. That's when Jack convinced himself it was for the best to stop trying and let the proverbial sleeping dogs lie.

'First thing I heard she'd gone to London and struggled to get a job at first. She's one of the smartest people I know but dropped out of school at sixteen because it bored her. Somehow she got in with an estate agent and met an American in the same business who convinced her to take a chance and go to work for him in Nashville.'

'But weddings? That strikes me as ironic when she couldn't wait to dump you.'

Despite his rekindled pain Jack

couldn't help smiling. Trust Rosie's daughter to tell things exactly like they were.

'I'm not sure.' The glossy Wedding Wishes website skimmed over Rosie's background simply mentioning her English heritage but nothing about any family connections. It emphasised her 20-plus years of experience in the 'location and experience sourcing business': 'Let Wedding Wishes bring your dreams to life!'

'Did she never contact us again?'

The word 'us' forced him to swallow the emotions swamping him before he could speak again. He'd never wrapped his head around her complete defection. To leave their youthful strained marriage hurt enough but to ignore their daughter's birthdays and Christmases her whole life? Never to ask for a photograph or seemingly care how Lisa was doing?

Jack had recognised Rosie's utter panic when the midwife had placed Lisa in her arms but he'd been overwhelmed too by the awesome responsibility and guessed most new parents felt the same way.

'No.' He struggled for a gentle way to explain the mystery and one throwaway phrase she tossed at him as she walked out of the door had always stuck. 'She said we were better off without her because she was a lousy wife and a hopeless mother.' Jack's voice turned to gravel and he swiped at his eyes, desperate not to break down.

'And was she?' Lisa's angry plea made him look up and Rosie's stubborn expression stared right back.

'She wasn't great,' he admitted, 'but I wasn't much of a husband or father either. We were young and stumbling our way to making a life together.' Jack grasped his daughter's hands. 'At least I thought we were. I believed we could tough it out and make it work.'

'But she didn't.' The flat statement lanced through him and he'd have done almost anything to contradict her but refused to lie.

'I suspect she suffered from post-natal depression but nobody recognised it so she never got any help.'

'That's sad if it's true but . . . '

'Doesn't make it any easier. I know.'

'Gino thinks I'm asking for trouble if I contact her.' Lisa straightened in the chair and pulled her hands back in her lap. 'Do you agree?'

He hesitated. The balance trick of supporting his daughter without admitting that deep down he sided with her fiancé might be beyond his ability.

'You're stressed out with the wedding. We all are. Maybe it's better to wait until after your honeymoon before you decide.'

'My dad. The eternal peacemaker. Pity you couldn't use your skills on my mother years ago.'

Jack let the sarcasm go. Lisa didn't realise the clueless, naive boy he'd been then. The idea that he could have given his young wife emotional support was laughable.

'Don't you think she'd find it ironic

that you're a divorce mediator these days?' Lisa's deep throaty laugh broke through. 'Sorry. Family mediator — as if that's supposed to sound better. We'll do it your way. For now.

'I'm off out with my bridesmaids. And don't for a minute think it's a hen night with an excess of cheap booze and me wearing a tacky L-plate and veil from the pound shop. We're having a nice meal at the Taj Majal followed by an early night.'

Jack smiled inwardly at how many of his genes she'd inherited. They both enjoyed company and having fun, although he did distinctly less of it these days, but knew where to draw the line. The young Rosie hadn't been as circumspect.

That's why he had been drawn to her. She was everything he wasn't — a fan of pushing the boundaries and shocking people. He often thought she agreed to his marriage proposal because no-one expected her to do anything so conventional. Her father refused to give his permission at first saying sixteen was too young for Rosie to know her own mind but gave in when she threatened to run away with Jack.

'Where's Gino?'

'His parents arrived this afternoon.' She wrinkled her nose. 'Remember we've got the family lunch tomorrow at the Old Goose. I wish now we'd picked a better time of year for the wedding. The Rossis won't be impressed by dreary, rain-soaked Fowey in the middle of winter.'

Jack held off saying I told you so. The evening she FaceTimed him from Rome to show off her stunning diamond ring was when Lisa insisted they'd get married on the weekend closest to Valentine's Day.

'Don't worry too much,' Jack reassured his daughter. 'The food's some of the best in Cornwall.' The smile returned to her face. 'Off you go. I might pop over and see your gran.'

'I think you'll find Wednesday is her Zumba night.' Lisa smirked and pushed back her chair. 'If you catch her, give her a kiss from me and say we'll pick her up tomorrow about six.' She rolled her eyes. 'I hope she doesn't wear that red gypsy dress and the gold shoes.'

His strong, determined mother never let her age stop her doing anything — in fact the older she got the less Eliza Kitto cared about what anybody thought. Jack needed a dose of her wisdom tonight.

★　★　★

'So tell us all about life in exotic Nashville.' Pam broke through the semblance of politeness they'd clung on to through teatime. With everybody's cups refilled, Rosie wouldn't be allowed to escape any time soon. 'I barely recognised you at the funeral.'

Rosie couldn't say the same in return because her cousin had hardly changed — apart from a few extra pounds on the hips and some fine lines around her mouth and eyes which struck Rosie as the result of smiling as opposed to stress.

Between Pam's job at a garden centre and running around after her three grown-up children who all lived locally she clearly stayed healthy and content with her life.

'I'll take a wild guess you haven't eaten a pasty in decades.'

If she admitted that her nutritionist and personal trainer would throw up their hands in horror she'd be laughed out of Cornwall.

'They're impossible to buy where I live.'

'Make your own. You enjoyed baking in the old days,' Pam persisted. 'Remember whipping up butterfly buns in Mum's kitchen for the village show?'

'I don't have the time now.' Rosie shrugged. 'It's not worth the effort for just me.'

'Why didn't you marry again?'

Rosie sensed everyone's attention on her. 'I thought you might've wanted more children?'

Tears welled up but Rosie blinked them back.

'She's a very successful business-woman.' Her mother reached across to squeeze Rosie's hand. 'It's difficult to work such long hours and cope with a family as well.'

'How about a glass of sherry before you leave?' Aunt Viv frowned at her older sister. 'We're so pleased to see young Rosie again. Don't take no notice of Pam, she gets on her high horse . . .'

'I'm only repeating what you all said before they arrived.' Heat blossomed on her cousin's round cheeks. 'We're supposed to be family and she was like a sister to me.' Pam jabbed a finger at Rosie.

'Sisters don't cut you dead for all these years and swan back in dressed like Lady Muck pretending nothing's happened.'

Rosie didn't consider today's dark green cashmere jumper, boot cut dark jeans and soft leather boots overly fancy but the obvious quality stood out among a room full of ordinary high street fashions.

'We'll skip the sherry if Mum doesn't mind too much. We've got a good hour drive back to our B&B and the rain's bad again.'

'What are your plans for tomorrow?' Aunt Viv wasn't going to let them slip away easily.

'We've booked a room in Fowey for the rest of the week.' They picked the pretty coastal town because it was close to St Wenn if they decided to visit but far enough away so they shouldn't bump into anyone they knew.

'It'd be nice to meet for lunch.'

'Some of us have to work,' Pam complained before an immediate hot blush lit up her face and neck. No doubt her mother suggested it for that very reason. 'I'm sure I can get the time off. Business is quiet this time of year and I'm owed several days.'

Rosie suppressed a smile at her cousin's defiance. Stubbornness ran in the Trethewey family.

'I've been checking on a few places for possible tie-ins with my business and I keep seeing the Old Goose mentioned. Would that do?'

'Would that do?' Pam snorted. 'You'll be lucky to get a table, even in the middle of winter. The chef's a celebrity now after winning one of those fancy cooking programmes. The food's supposed to be awesome.'

'How about you leave it to me and I'll see what I can manage? If it doesn't pan out I'll find somewhere else and give you a call later to fix a meeting time.' Ignoring her cousin's disdainful expression wasn't easy. 'Are you ready, Mum?'

They gathered up their belongings.

'Thanks for tea, Pam, it was lovely.' Rosie offered another olive branch.

'How would you know? You ate two bites of sausage roll and pushed the rest around your plate.'

'I didn't realise I was being scrutinised.' Rosie struggled to make a joke while curling up inside. 'Tomorrow I'll make sure to stuff myself where you can clearly see.' The barb hit home and her cousin's blush intensified. 'Bye, everyone.' Right now Rosie didn't care if she never saw any of them again.

'Come here, love.' Out of the blue, Aunt Viv threw her arms around Rosie, surrounding her with the familiar scent of lily of the valley etched in Rosie's childhood memories. 'Pam missed you something awful.'

'I missed her too.'

'I know. Off you go and make sure you drive careful. You're not used to our narrow roads and it's nasty out there.'

Now Rosie would spend the rest of the evening putting up with her mum's sympathy and praying the internet worked.

Two hours later her mother snored in the background while Rosie stared at one of yesterday's emails in disbelief.

In For a Penny...

'Tie or no tie?' Jack held the dark blue silk tie up to his freshly ironed blue and white striped shirt for his daughter's opinion.

'No tie.' Lisa snatched it away. 'This is supposed to be a casual lunch for you to get to know each other.' Lisa's laughing gaze swept over him. 'You're nervous. I've never seen you nervous before.'

How to explain to his gorgeous, confident daughter that he was petrified of letting her down? It reminded him of Lisa's first day at school when he fussed over every last detail until it drove his mother crazy.

'Don't try so hard,' Eliza had said. 'The new mothers dropping their kids off are just as wary as you and they aren't perfect parents either. There's no such thing.'

'Didn't Gran sort you out last night?' Lisa threw across a lightweight navy jumper for him to put on instead of the grey tweed sports coat he'd planned to wear.

'Yes,' Jack admitted, 'or at least she tried.'

'Did you run by her my idea about contacting my mother?'

He hesitated, close to confessing the truth but with no reply from Rosie he upheld up his promise to Gino and stuck with nodding.

'Don't tell me I suppose she agreed with you?' Lisa flopped on the bed, giving him an appraising stare.

'Well, yes, she did.' After a long verbal battle Eliza had caved when he pressed Gino's case that his fiancée had enough on her mind until after they got through the wedding. Jack hurried to drag on his jumper and straighten his tousled hair. 'We ought to go to your gran's now. You know she won't be ready and we'll have to chivvy her along.'

'Fine.' Lisa stood and gave her hair a quick toss, checking her golden mane in the mirror. The gesture was Rosie to a T and was like a knife in Jack's heart. 'See you downstairs.' She ran her fingers over his freshly shaved jaw. 'You missed a bit.' With a playful skip she danced out of the room.

If he could take back the email he'd rashly sent, Jack would. He crossed his fingers and hoped Rosie's silence would hold.

* * *

Why now after 25 years? Rosie didn't need to reread Jack's email because the words were engraved on her brain. Beside her, Maggie smiled out of the car window enjoying today's dry weather and seemingly oblivious to the turmoil in her daughter's head. First thing this morning Rosie claimed a headache and sent her mother down to breakfast alone while she considered whether or not to reply to Jack's shocking message. By eight o'clock she came down on the side of 'not'.

'Hello, Rosie. I'm sorry to break my promise not to contact you but Lisa has suddenly expressed an interest in getting in touch with you and I didn't want it to come as a complete shock if she does.

'Our little girl is getting married on Saturday to a fine young man from Rome called Gino Rossi and his parents asked about you which got her thinking more, I suppose. Gino and I persuaded her not to rush into deciding anything until after they return from honeymoon. If you want to pre-empt her that's up to you but I don't want her upset this week.'

What could Rosie say? Nothing. There was no reasonable explanation for her behaviour and what was done was done. Her busy life left no space for a grown-up daughter who resented her and wanted to harangue her absent mother. She didn't need Lisa to ladle on even more guilt than she'd heaped on herself over the years.

Rosie's satnav told her to take the next right turn and she switched her attention back to the road.

'We're nearly at our hotel, Mum.' The Heron's Nest should suit her mother's tastes and might also be a perfect addition to her British portfolio.

Her clients came in two divergent groups — those who wanted the biggest, flashiest wedding with every conceivable extravagance and the complete opposite type who sought the most intimate and unique experience possible.

She could market the boutique hotel as perfect for fans of British literature. The Heron's Nest sat across the road from Ferryside, Daphne du Maurier's holiday home and within a short driving distance of Menabilly the inspiration for Manderley.

Lovers of Kenneth Grahame's 'Wind In The Willows' could visit the Fowey Hotel and see the original letters telling his young son charming stories based around the river which later became his famous books.

Rosie eased around the last sharp corner and gasped.

'Wow!' The pictures on the website didn't do justice to the jewel of a building, tucked in a bend in the river and shimmering in the pale wintry sunshine.

She admired the uneven whitewashed walls, dark red shutters and baskets of colourful winter pansies hanging either side of the solid dark wood door and set off by gleaming freshly polished brass. A wisp of smoke trailed from the chimney towards the clear blue sky and everything about the Heron's Nest beamed out a warm welcome.

'It's some pretty.' Maggie smiled. 'No wonder you're good at your job. You knew what would suit us.'

The rare praise touched Rosie and she couldn't hide her pleasure.

'Let's hope it's as good inside.' Rosie had been fooled before. Outward appearances didn't necessarily match what lurked under the surface. Jack didn't fall in that category because he was the most straightforward man she'd ever come across. Don't go there now, she told herself.

'If you'd like to get out I'll fetch our bags.' She hurried to open the boot, suppressing a grin over mentally naming it that way after 20-plus years of referring to the trunk of a car. Maybe some things were so ingrained even 4,000 miles and half a lifetime couldn't erase them.

'If you can't face Pam and all of them again I'll go on my own,' Maggie offered.

'It's not a problem.' Rosie locked the car and gave a careless shrug. 'In for a penny in for a pound as y'all say here.'

'You sounded like a proper Yank then. It's the first time I've really picked up on it.'

'Are you the Trethewey ladies?' A smiling young woman bustled down the path to greet them wiping her hands on her jeans before holding one out. 'I'm Demelza Stephens, the owner. And no, my husband's unfortunately not a glowering hunk named Ross.' Engaging dimples popped out on either side of her mouth.

'He's an even-tempered history teacher called Andy. I'm in the middle of making scones which explains the floury handshake.'

Friendly welcome. Soft Cornish accent. Home baking. Rosie could sell this place standing on her head.

Demelza showed them around the sprawling 18th-century house loaded with lovingly polished family antiques.

'I know you're off out to lunch soon but I'll happily bring a tray of tea or coffee to your room while you freshen up. Which would you prefer?

Rosie chose coffee as her mother opted for tea.

'One of each coming up.' Demelza handed over the heavy old-fashioned key. 'Do you need any help with your bags? You're at the top of the stairs on the right. It's en-suite.'

'We're good, thanks.' Rosie led the way and managed to wrangle the luggage and the key to get into their room. She instantly pictured a newly-wed couple closing the door behind them, wrapping their arms around each other and gazing at the view out over the tranquil river while wondering how they got so lucky.

'Careful, Rosalind dear, you're in danger of sounding romantic,' Crispin would have said. The thought almost made her laugh aloud. In Wedding Wishes she provided the steady business brain while her artistic partner dealt with the starry-eyed aspect of their clients' desires.

'I'm putting my feet up for half an hour,' Maggie declared, slipping off her shoes and stretching out on one of the twin beds.

A quiet tap on the door stirred Rosie from her musings and she relieved their landlady of a loaded tray.

'Is it far to the Old Goose?'

'About a five or ten-minute walk.' Demelza frowned. 'I doubt you'll get in. Even this time of year they're always busy. I suppose you might get lucky if you don't mind waiting.'

'Oh, we've got a reservation.'

'Wow, good for you. We go once a year on our anniversary and book up then for the next one.'

Rosie didn't explain that she'd pulled strings with the chef through one of her London contacts. The promise of promoting the Old Goose in her business went a long way.

'You'll love it. I'll see you later. Beds to make. Washing to do.' Demelza disappeared back downstairs.

Rosie considered waking Maggie but a short nap would do her mother good. Checking emails wasn't an option in case of more unwelcome messages. Rosie poured herself a cup of coffee and decided to enjoy a few minutes doing absolutely nothing.

★ ★ ★

Glancing around the table, Jack sensed his solitariness more keenly than usual and caught his mother's wistful smile as she read his mind. Did the fact she lost his father a decade ago and Eliza's inborn sense of independence lessen the feeling of loneliness or did none of that matter?

The evident, easy companionship between Gino's long-married parents and the shining new love shared by the soon-to-be newlyweds emphasised his own lack of success in that department.

Rationally he understood being alone was better than life with the wrong partner but still drained the glass of wine faster than he should.

'Earth to Daddy.' Lisa's amused voice penetrated his musing. 'Signor Rossi's asked you the same question at least six times.'

'Oh, I'm sorry.' He pushed aside his uneaten mussels.

'What you will do with yourself when this lovely girl is living and working in

Rome?' Salvatore's expansive smile irritated Jack.

'Of course I'll miss her but it's hardly the other side of the world and there are plenty of cheap flights these days.' He forced out a laugh. 'You'll find it hard to get rid of me.'

'We'll come back often, Daddy.' Lisa's soft hand wrapped over his almost finished him.

'I know, sweetheart.' His self-pity faded and he mentally patted himself on the back. He'd done a fine job bringing up his exceptional daughter and defied anyone to disagree.

'I don't believe it. The Prodigal returns.'

Jack glanced at his white-faced mother, her mouth gaping open as she stared behind him.

Awkward Conspiracy

Rosie met her former mother-in-law's incredulous stare as the bottom dropped out of her world.

'Mummy?' A girl's crystal clear anguished voice rang out and an unnatural hush descended on the crowded restaurant.

The sight of Lisa a few metres away, and far lovelier than the newspaper cutting hinted at, stunned Rosie.

'Keep walking,' Pam whispered. 'Go over to her. You don't have any choice.'

Rosie wanted to plead that of course she did because turning right around and walking out seemed an extremely viable option right now.

Suddenly Jack loomed in front of her, his boyish features transformed into an attractive rugged handsomeness with age. The dark blue eyes she'd drowned in as a smitten teenager weren't sparkling today.

'Come outside with me.' He grasped her arm. 'Lisa doesn't need to meet you again in the middle of all this lot.'

Normally in control, Rosie couldn't even nod her agreement, let alone speak. She allowed him to lead her towards the willowy blonde being comforted by a dark-haired stranger, presumably the prospective bride-groom. Jack jerked his head towards the French doors and the other man got the hint so they somehow ended up in the garden.

'I didn't think you were one for surprises, Daddy, but you pulled this off perfectly.' A wide smile split Lisa's beautiful face in two. 'This is absolutely the best wedding present.'

'We weren't sure you'd think so.' Rosie rushed to agree and ignored Jack's surprise. 'I hope I haven't spoiled your family lunch?'

'Absolutely not. You'll have to join us, won't she, Daddy?'

'Of course.' His mechanical response held nothing in the way of warmth. 'I'll go in and see if they can put us all together to eat.'

'No. You stay here and I will go.' The young man flashed Rosie a bewitching dark-eyed smile. Considerate and charming weren't qualities to be sneezed at.

The three of them stood in an uncomfortable silence and Rosie drank in the sight of her beautiful baby all grown up. Lisa wore an elegant black and white two piece Rosie recognised as by Mauro Gasperi, a favourite designer among younger Italians who craved style at affordable prices.

'If you'd prefer it I'm happy to go, too?' The words hardly left Jack's mouth before both women snapped a quick 'No'. A slow smile crept over his sombre expression igniting a long-forgotten flutter in the pit of Rosie's stomach.

'Lisa, how about if your . . . mother comes around to the house tonight for a proper chat? If there's time in the schedule.' His playful wink did more funny things to Rosie's insides. 'The wedding plans are in a folder this thick.'

Throwing his hands wide apart he tipped back his head and laughed. The same deep, warm spontaneous sound she'd managed to blot out until now.

'And spreadsheets? Don't get me started.'

'It's important to cover every detail if you want the day to go smoothly.' Rosie's defence made her daughter smile.

'See, Daddy it's not just me. M . . . I mean, she understands.' The stumble over what name to call her stung but Rosie didn't blame Lisa for the reticence.

'We can still have lunch together now if you want?' Rosie ventured. 'That is, if your handsome fiancé worked his magic.'

'Isn't he adorable?' Lisa beamed.

'He sure is. You've got good taste.'

'Must be inherited.' Her cheeks burned. 'I mean . . . '

'It's OK.' Rosie dared to brush a light touch over her daughter's hand, objectively noticing the long slender fingers matching her own. 'Your father's always been a handsome man. It's unfair the way most men age better than women.'

'That's not true.' Jack's outburst made her smile. 'You were a pretty girl but now you're . . . ' He lowered his eyes.

'All set.' Gino leaned out around the door.

'Did I see Maggie come in with you?'

'My other grandmother is here?' Lisa squealed.

'Yes and my cousin Pam, Auntie Viv and Uncle Greg.' Her daughter's bright smile wobbled.

'But we can forget doing this if it's too much. We didn't think it through really did we, Jack?' She silently begged him to go along with the charade.

Trained to read body language and negotiate between what people say and what they actually mean, Jack failed when faced with the new glossy version of his ex-wife. Maybe he never understood her in the first place?

But before the words 'This is a huge mistake' could slip out of his mouth, Rosie smiled. A hesitant smile, matching the one she slid in his direction at the Polvennor school drama club, inched across her face and Jack fell in love with Rosalind Anne Trethewey for the second time in his life.

'No. No, we didn't.'

'We should all go and sit down.' Gino nudged his elbow. 'As you say here, we are making a spectacle of ourselves. Very odd expression — but what do I know?'

Later, Jack would be sure to thank the young man because without his quick reactions they'd still be floundering.

'Good idea.' Jack cleared his throat and plastered on a smile, hoping to convince their family audience with his long dormant acting skills.

'Lisa, I'm sure Maggie would love to sit between you and Gino.' His former mother-in-law hadn't taken her eyes off Lisa and it plainly took all her self-control not to throw her arms around her long-lost granddaughter.

Rosie mustn't end up anywhere near the inquisitive Rossis before they could synchronise their stories. Wherever she ended up held the potential for calamity so it became a question of which place might cause the least amount of damage.

'We'll all sit together down the other end of the table.' Rosie gestured around to her other relatives, none trying to hide their curiosity at this unexpected development in their lunch plans.

'Good idea.'

'I thought it might be.' Her low, husky response threaded with a hint of amusement set off a flash of longing in Jack to whisk her out of here before challenging her as to what she thought she was playing at — before kissing her until their heads spun.

Kiss her. Are you out of your mind?

He couldn't believe he had even thought it.

'Jack, sit here.' Eliza pointed to Lisa's vacant seat and treated him to one of her rare stern glares. Normally an easygoing mother she nevertheless possessed an unbending sense of right and wrong.

Lying to cover up for his ex-wife's bizarre reappearance fell firmly into the 'wrong' category. The fact he was a grown man made no difference.

The waitress took everyone's orders and thankfully the conversations drifting Jack's way sounded reasonable, mainly about the unpredictable weather and the upcoming wedding. He relaxed back in the chair and refilled his wine glass.

'You didn't know she was coming any more than the man in the moon.' Eliza kept her voice low, a rare occurrence for his outspoken mother. 'That girl always had you wrapped around her finger.' He didn't try to argue but succumbed to a half-smile. 'It's not funny.'

'No, Mum. I really am sorry.'

'For lying or falling for her batting eyelashes again?'

'Rosie never batted an eyelash in her life.'

Eliza rolled her eyes.

'Men. You're all blind as bats. Don't fall for her wiles, son. She'll jet off back to America in a minute and you'll be a mess again.' The clear message flashed in big neon letters over her head: 'I can't pick up the pieces a second time.'

'I admit it's a shock seeing Rosie again but I promise I won't do anything daft.'

'I've heard that one before,' his mother scoffed.

Out of the corner of his eye Jack caught Maggie Trethewey's bright flushed smile. Of all the people in this equation she'd perhaps come off the worst being left behind to bear the brunt of the incessant gossip when her daughter ran away.

The village labelled Jack the innocent party — a brave young boy left to bring up a tiny baby alone — and his young wife 'no better than she should be'. He could've helped by including them in Lisa's childhood but shut his mind and door to Rosie's family.

He popped a potato in his mouth but they'd gone cold while he talked. The irony of coming to one of the best restaurants in Cornwall and ignoring the food didn't escape him. Everyone else seemed to have finished eating.

'Does anyone fancy a quick walk around Fowey?' Gino looked hopefully around the long table. 'It's not raining.'

'That's an awesome idea.' Rosie pushed her chair back but didn't rush to stand when no-one else moved. 'Mum?' Her voice throbbed with nerves and despite himself Jack felt sorry for her.

'I'm a bit tired, love,' Maggie said. 'You go ahead if you like and your aunt and I can find a café for a cup of tea and a natter.'

'I'll come.' Pam's forceful response brought a flush of heat to Rosie's cheeks and Jack guessed there was unfinished business between the cousins. Years ago they were best friends, more like sisters really, but presumably that fell by the wayside when his ex-wife fled her Cornish life.

'We would be happy to join Signora Trethewey if that is OK?' Salvatore patted his wife's hand. 'Ariana is liking the British tea very much.'

In the general rush of finding everyone's coats and getting ready to leave Jack found himself standing by Rosie.

'Walk or café?' Her low, raspy whisper brought him back to being sixteen and searching for the courage to ask Rosie out, unable to believe she fancied him.

Out of the blue she'd volunteered to help backstage at the drama club and Jack's friends teased that it was obvious where her sudden urge to paint scenery came from. Rosie got tired of waiting and cornered him after the dress rehearsal to see if he'd take her to see the new Indiana Jones film. The rest was history.

'I suspect a dose of fresh air might help us both.' Her voice brought him back to earth.

She slipped her hand through his arm and a waft of familiar perfume surprised him. Despite her glossy new look did she seriously still wear the same inexpensive floral scent? Once when he described it poetically as reminiscent of late season roses blossoming in the sunshine she had roared with laughter.

'Oh, Jack, it's the cheapest one Boots sells.'

He suspected this modern version cost a whole lot more — rather like her whole appearance these days. His mother's warning filtered in but he chose to push it away. No way would he make a fool of himself over Rosie again. He'd learned his lesson the hard way.

Change of Heart

All of this was her mother's fault. So much for their agreed plan to hang around outside the church on Saturday before fading away unnoticed. Rosie plastered on a smile.

'By the way, Jack, do you remember Pam?'

Her cousin snorted.

'Of course he remembers me. For heaven's sake, we were all in school together. Who do you think helped out by babysitting Lisa so Jack could go back to college?'

'You did?' The punches kept on coming. A vivid picture of Pam cradling Rosie's baby stung like antiseptic on a raw wound.

'Yep, I often took care of her when his mum was busy. Lisa took her first steps in our front room.'

'Leave it, Pam, please.' Jack's gentle

remonstrance touched her. 'What's done is done and I'd say Lisa turned out pretty well.'

'No thanks to me.'

'Rosie, that's not what I meant . . . '

'Don't you dare apologise.' Her face flamed. 'You've every right to be proud of her. She's an amazing woman and that's all down to you.'

'You're still her mother.' Jack caressed his warm hand along the curve of her cheek and against all sense she stared into his amazing eyes, the darkest blue of a midnight sea on a clear winter's night.

'No. I'm not.' She pulled away, determined not to succumb to his undeniable draw. 'I gave birth to Lisa. End of story. A proper mother nurtures and protects her child.' Tears trickled down her face and Rosie angrily brushed them away. 'I failed her.'

'You weren't much more than a child yourself.' Pam grasped her shoulder. 'Don't be so hard on yourself.

'Why the sudden change of heart? A

minute ago you were berating me.'

'I've been making this all about me and my feelings which isn't right. I wanted to help you at the time but you pushed me away.'

'If I hadn't left I'd have fallen apart.' Rosie's voice broke.

'None of us knew what to do,' Jack murmured, 'me least of all.'

He knew before she did. One endless night when Lisa couldn't be consoled he had walked their baby girl around the house for hours until she flaked out in his arms. Jack set her back in her cot before joining Rosie in bed.

'You can't do this, can you? Her. Me. Where will you go? How will you manage?' he'd pleaded.

Keeping her back turned away from him she'd pretended to be asleep until he gave up and left her alone.

'Anyway, what happens next?'

Pam's question startled her.

'In what way?'

'Is this the last time we see you?'

'I don't know.'

'You don't know?'

'I'm trying to be honest. Let's walk on a bit further or Lisa and Gino will think we're old and lazy.' Rosie threw Jack a silent plea for help while realising she'd no right to ask.

'Excellent idea. It's bad enough having a daughter old enough to get married without completely giving in to middle age.

'As a bonus, I happen to know the whereabouts of the best ice-cream shop that stays open all winter.' Jack looped an arm around each woman and Rosie noticed patches of light blue peeping through the grey overcast sky as a gentle breeze blew in off the river.

They weren't the only people making the most of the dry weather for a stroll around the small town.

'And this is important — why?' Pam teased. 'We've just finished lunch at one of Cornwall's best restaurants.'

'Yeah, and no offence to the Old Goose but I couldn't enjoy a single mouthful,' Rosie admitted. 'Plus ice-cream is my weakness.' She caught her cousin's barely veiled surprise and determined to cram down the largest cone on offer if it killed her.

'Fine. Ninety-nines all around with clotted cream on top.' The unmistakable challenge made Rosie's heart sink. 'I didn't finish my fancy fish and chips because Mum kept nattering and asking idiotic questions. Dad grouched about the cost for what he called tarted up bits of food.' Pam smiled at Jack.

'And that's despite the fact you made it clear you were treating us. The counselling business must be doing well if you can afford all this.

'I heard Lisa telling about the ton of exotic flowers she's ordered to decorate the church, the fancy reception you've got planned at Rashleigh Grange — and not forgetting her designer wedding dress . . . '

'Give it a break, Pam,' Rosie chided her cousin. 'For a start it's no-one else's business what a wedding costs outside of the people paying for it and how do you know Lisa and Gino aren't contributing? Lots of young people do these days.'

'You don't need to defend me, either.' Jack's face and neck burned a bright crimson. 'I refuse to apologise or explain for spoiling my daughter.' He tossed a smile Rosie's way. 'Don't take this the wrong way but Lisa didn't have the easiest of times growing up one way and another and it's my joy and privilege to give her the best send off possible into her new life.'

'I'm sorry. Truly sorry. I was out of line.' Pam shook her head. 'No offence but I'll give the ice-cream a miss and go track down Mum and Dad. I need to head on home before the kids get off school.' Her wary expression unsettled Rosie. 'You're welcome to pop over if you've got time before you leave.'

'Thanks. I'll see how things go.' On impulse, she flung her arms around her cousin who stiffened before relaxing into the impromptu hug. 'It's great to get together again, it really is.'

Spending the last couple of weeks with her mother and reconnecting with the rest of her family threw a spotlight on the emptiness of her Nashville life. Rosie's limited non-work time was spent either in the gym or attending board meetings or charity functions for helping troubled teenagers.

The gym fell under the heading of essential to maintaining her health rather than genuine pleasure but working with young people brought a deep satisfaction. But was all of that enough?

'Take care of yourself, Rosiebug.' Pam's childhood name for her slipped out and loosened the tears Rosie had fought so hard to control.

'Off you go.' Half-pushing her cousin away, Rosie collapsed into Jack's outstretched arms, comforted by his reassuring warmth.

Clinging on to him until she managed to catch her breath, she glanced up to meet his deep blue eyes brimming over with an emotion she couldn't put a name to. She could still easily reach around his back but as her hands ran down over his jumper Rosie recognised solid muscles that didn't exist at eighteen.

'I'm not a scrawny boy any more.' Jack touched her hair. 'We've both changed.'

'For the better? Counsellor? What's all that about?'

'Rosie, I . . . '

'Daddy, we've been waiting for you. Hurry up.' Lisa tugged on his sleeve and pointed to her watch. 'I've sent Gino over to the café to round up the wrinklies.

'Remember I'm seeing the florist at five and then um . . . you're coming around, aren't you?' She stumbled over what to call Rosie and Jack couldn't imagine how that made her feel.

'Hey, don't worry about it. You've got less than forty-eight hours before the big day and no doubt you've a ton to do. We can catch up another time.'

'Can we?' The sharp question pierced the immediate, awkward silence. 'Is that a promise?' Lisa tossed her ponytail and Jack grimaced.

Ninety-nine percent of the time his daughter was the sweetest person on the planet but the final one percent brought a similarity to Jekyll and Hyde. The shock and initial excitement at seeing her mother had faded to allow reality in with a vengeance. 'Oh, how could I forget? You break those.'

'Don't talk to your . . . '

'She is not my mother! She merely gave birth to me.'

'That's . . . '

'No, Jack, she's right.' Rosie pushed his arms away and straightened her shoulders. 'I should've listened to my instincts instead of my soft-hearted mother and stayed well away from Cornwall. All I've done is upset everyone.' A tremble ran through her voice.

'I wish you well on Saturday and for the rest of your life. Gino is a wonderful man and I'm sure you'll be very happy together.' Rosie tugged the belt on her soft purple coat in around her slender waist. 'I'm off to track down my mum. You've got my contact details if you ever need to get in touch.'

'But . . . '

'You don't need me to stay around and mess things up again.' She touched his bare wrist and the brush of her cold fingers sent shivers through Jack's blood. 'Knowing when to quit. It's an important lesson I learned the hard way.' Rosie brushed a tender kiss over his cheek. 'Take care of yourself.' The whispered request was barely audible.

'You too.' Letting her go the first time was heartbreaking but this was worse because second chances only happened in fairy stories. Jack watched his old love walk briskly away and never turn to look back.

'Daddy, I . . . '

'Don't.' He patted her arm. 'Just don't, sweetheart. I understand.'

'I know you do.' Tears welled in

Lisa's deep smoky eyes, so much the image of her mother's. 'When I saw her in the Old Goose earlier I thought it was Christmas morning and no-one told me.

'But the more I let myself think I remembered all the nights I cried myself to sleep wondering why she didn't care enough to even send a birthday card.' She gulped back a sob. 'I can't get past that.'

'I'm not sure if it helps but I used to cry, too.' Jack admitted and his stomach knotted with a deep gut-wrenching pain. 'You used to ask me over and over for an explanation and what could I say? I always dreaded you getting the idea that you weren't good enough to make her stay.'

'Instead you took all the blame. That wasn't fair.'

'It was the least I could do.' He shrugged it off. 'We were too young for marriage and the responsibility of a baby.'

'You coped.'

The last thing Lisa needed was him going into counsellor mode so Jack chose his words carefully.

'We're all different. You know that.' He mentally took a step back. 'I believe we've got a florist to see, young lady.'

'We certainly do.' She smacked a loud kiss on his forehead. 'You're the best. We'll meet you at the car.'

A weary heaviness weighed Jack down. He had buried the dream of rekindling his family long ago — until today when Rosie barrelled back into his life with her big ideas, wide smile and sparkling eyes. The girl never knew how to leave well alone.

Drawing a line under his love for Rosie Trethewey was smart so why the sweep of sadness running through him?

No Time to Lose

'Are you all right, love?'

All right? Was her mother out of her mind? A shudder ran through Rosie and she struggled to hide her distress. Having a breakdown in the middle of the Wooden Spoon café would put the lid on one of the worst days ever.

'Have you finished your tea?' she asked Maggie.

'Yes, your aunt and uncle left with Pam and Lisa's young man came for the Rossis. Gino's lovely you know, he said . . . '

'Why don't you tell me when we get back to the hotel?' Rosie yanked Maggie's coat off the back of the chair and held it out for her to put on. The sympathy pouring from her mother's gentle eyes almost finished her off. 'Have you paid?

'Pam treated us.'

'Let's go.' Rosie threw open the door and the blast of fresh air cooled off her flash of panic. 'It's a bit late now to leave today but if it's OK with you we'll head back to Watford in the morning. I'm sorry you'll miss the wedding.'

Without giving her mother a chance to answer she practically sprinted down the road before slowing about halfway along to check on Maggie.

Now languishing several metres behind she'd turned red-faced with the effort of trying to keep up. So much for Rosie's intention to be a better daughter.

She should have returned to Nashville straight after her dad's funeral and none of this would have happened. Rather than running back to embarrass her mother she stood still and pretended to study a red dress hanging in a shop window.

'It wouldn't suit you.'

'You're right.' They both know she'd never consider wearing the cheap design held together with gaudy sequins and obviously aimed at the Valentine's Day date market.

'Gino said our Lisa was a bit uptight after lunch.'

Not facing each other made it easier to hide her emotions and Rosie rolled her shoulders in a casual shrug.

'All brides get the jitters. She'll come around,' Maggie said.

'I doubt it, Mum, and I don't blame her.' Rosie's blunt acceptance of the impossible situation drew a heavy sigh from her mother. 'Come on, it's getting chilly. Let's get back to the Heron's Nest where it's good and warm.' She linked her arm through Maggie's. 'It's OK. I'll get over it. Life goes on.'

Half an hour later they sat in silence as both waited for the other to speak first. Neither of them showed any interest in the hot drinks now cooling on the table, courtesy of Demelza who insisted on bringing them a tray partly to pump Rosie for her opinion on the Old Goose.

Rosie stared out of the window,

vaguely registering the fresh rain splatters on the salt-stained glass.

''She is not my mother! She merely gave birth to me.' Those were her exact words.'

'Oh, love, I'm so sorry.'

'Me, too.' The admission of disappointment was dragged out of her by sheer weariness. Next thing, Rosie dissolved in tears and buried her head in her mother's shoulder. Being consoled like a small child touched something deep inside and a quarter-century's worth of suppressed anguish gushed out.

Along with the seemingly unstoppable tears came stories of sleepless nights spent pacing around her lonely bedsit in a rough part of London, wondering if her baby was crying for her, too. Many times she considered jumping on the train back to Cornwall and pleading for Jack's forgiveness.

'Once I even bought a ticket and got as far as the platform before tearing it up and running out of the station.'

Rosie's anguish was reflected in Maggie's sad expression.

'Didn't you ever meet any nice men over there in America?'

'Not really.' As if that would solve everything. 'Work took over and filled the gap. Time went on and . . . I got out of the habit of bothering.' Rosie managed a wry smile. 'Men seemed too much trouble and I'm not the internet dating sort.'

'You loved Jack.'

How did mothers do that every single time? Nail their children in a few pithy words by striking to the heart of what was wrong.

'I was sixteen when we got married. What did I know about love?'

'For a smart woman you can be some daft.' Maggie shook her head. 'Doesn't matter if you're six or sixty-six. You thought your father was a bit of a bully and he was a strong-minded man but . . .'

'He was your strong-minded man and loved you more than anything on earth. I get that now,' Rosie admitted. 'I see now it wasn't that Daddy couldn't forgive me for leaving Jack and Lisa but he couldn't bear how terribly it hurt you. He was a born fixer and it distressed him that he couldn't fix your pain.'

'There's nothing we can do about that now.'

'No.' Accepting failure wasn't her usual way but a sense of relief swept through Rosie because she didn't have to keep fighting this particular battle.

* * *

By nature Jack wasn't a moper but tonight not even Lisa's uplifted spirits once she plunged back into the wedding plans could cheer him.

'Take care of yourself.'

He suspected Rosie's parting words lay at the crux of his unusual gloom. For all these years he'd willingly taken care of Lisa and now surreptitiously looked out for his mother although she'd snort with laughter if he dared say that out loud.

Jack's mind kept drifting back to the first few months of his young marriage and the novelty of coming home from his dull job at the factory to find Rosie waiting with a kiss and a scraped-together meal. They were just kids playing at being grown up — until they discovered Rosie was expecting and the game came to an abrupt halt.

'Signor Jack, why are you sitting here in the dark?' Gino flicked on the light switch.

'Oh, sorry, I hadn't realised it was this late. Did your parents . . . enjoy lunch?' Jack's hesitation made Gino laugh and against the odds he found himself joining in. 'Heavens, I'm really sorry things got messed up.'

'They were surprised the food was so good.' A tinge of heat coloured Gino's olive complexion. 'Sorry — but we all know the reputation of British food around the rest of the world.'

Jack slipped off his reading glasses

and set down the newspaper he'd struggled to concentrate on reading.

'Let's be honest, the food was the least of our concerns.' He nodded towards the sideboard. 'I think this requires a decent single malt.'

'That is one habit I have happily picked up.' Gino fetched the bottle and a couple of glasses. Passing over a glass to Jack he took his own drink and claimed the chair by the window.

'Are you going to tell Lisa?'

'What about?'

Jack swirled the whisky and savoured the rich peaty aroma before taking the first sip.

'Oh, maybe the fact I'm not a wizard and didn't conjure Rosie out of thin air. If anything I tried to put her off.'

'I am not sure that it matters any longer. Lisa did not exactly rush to give her a wedding invitation.' Gino frowned. 'You seemed . . . no, it is none of my business.'

'Spit it out. We're family now or close enough.'

'I sensed there is still a connection between you and Signorina Trethewey.'

'History. Nothing more.' Staring down at the glass he avoided Gino's dark, perceptive eyes.

'Ah . . . of course.'

'You don't believe me?' One expressive Italian shrug gave the only answer Jack needed. 'Rosie was my first love.'

'And your last.'

'There's still time.' He attempted to crack a joke while remaining pretty sure Lisa had shared every detail of his non-existent love life with her fiancé.

'So there is.' Gino drained his glass. 'I should be going. Lisa thought she might be back from the final bridesmaids' council of war but I am guessing they opened another bottle of wine.' A wide grin creased his expressive face.

'I promised to have coffee with my parents and they are not late to bed these days.' He walked over to the door. 'I will shut my mouth after saying one more thing. I felt Signorina Rosalind's regret and yours too. Maybe think about it and do not wait until it is too late.'

The jangly strains of the 'Floral Dance', the Italian's new ringtone, interrupted making them both laugh. It was one of Lisa's good-humoured efforts to introduce her future husband to all things Cornish.

'*Il mio amore*.' Gino smiled and cradled the phone. 'Are you sure?' He threw Jack a panicked glance. 'Please put the television on the local news. Lisa says the Heron's Nest is on fire.'

After a fumble with the remote, Jack stared in disbelief at the horrific pictures of the burning building. Angry flames shot into the night sky and multiple fire engines surrounded the chaotic scene.

'Tell Lisa I'm leaving right away.'

'I'm coming, too,' Gino insisted before falling quiet. 'It's OK, my love, I will come for you.' He shoved his mobile back in his pocket. 'You go ahead. I will pick her up at the pub and we will follow.' Making a grasp for

Jack's shoulder he held him back. 'Drive with care. Lisa could not bear anything to happen to you.' The word 'too' hung unspoken between them.

Jack nodded and raced into the hall, barely stopping long enough to grab a heavy old coat and his car keys. Nothing mattered except not losing Rosie again.

Under the Same Roof

Despite the foil blanket tightened around her shoulders, Rosie shook with a mixture of sheer adrenaline and relief. How they'd escaped was nothing short of a miracle, something she'd stopped believing in until tonight.

Thank heavens her mother had made one of her night-time trips to the bathroom and spotted the flames.

'What are we going to do?' Maggie sobbed. 'We've nowhere to . . . '

'Mum, it's all right. We're fine and no-one's hurt. That's the main thing. The only thing that matters.' The words trotted out on autopilot while her brain raced. 'We'll call Auntie Viv or Pam. One of them will take us in.'

She spotted Demelza, white-faced and shaking, standing on the other side of the road and being comforted by her husband. Their own loss of a few clothes and her laptop ranked pitifully low in comparison.

The heartache of watching their life savings literally go up in smoke was unimaginable. It didn't matter how good the insurance payout was, it wouldn't bring back the ancient building.

Through the fire engine's flashing blue lights Rosie caught sight of a man arguing with a policeman and despite everything she cracked a smile. She'd recognise Jack's distinctive stance anywhere.

Rosie watched the policeman point towards them and Jack took off running, pushing other people out of the way in his haste.

'Oh, my goodness, are you all right?' He grabbed her by the shoulders, lifting Rosie off her feet in his panic.

'I'm fine. We're fine. Put me down. Please.' It took a second for her request to register but when it finally clicked, he set her gently back on the grass.

'Sorry.' Jack shoved a hand through

his unruly hair. 'Lisa saw the report of the fire on the local news and rang me. They're on the way.'

'Who are?'

'Lisa and Gino, of course.'

The same Lisa who couldn't wait to get rid of me earlier, Rosie thought.

'Do they know what caused the fire?'

'Not for certain but I get the impression they suspect faulty wiring. Thankfully everyone got out safely.'

'I'm sorry, Mrs Trethewey, I didn't mean to ignore you.' Jack stuttered out an apology to her mother. 'Hasn't anyone offered you somewhere to sit or a cup of tea?'

'Yes, they did, but we turned it down,' Rosie interrupted. 'Mum insisted on staying here.'

'Didn't seem right while those poor souls were watching their home burn.' Maggie nodded towards the hotel owners.

'There's a chance it won't be a complete loss.' Jack pointed to the smouldering roof. 'They might've caught it on time.'

'I hope so, for their sake.'

'Oh, Mum, thank goodness you're all right!'

Rosie staggered under the strength of Lisa's hug and for the first time since getting out of the smoke-filled building a tear trickled down her face. Relief overwhelmed her and it took every last ounce of control not to completely lose it. Her daughter let go and flung her arms around Maggie.

'I'm so glad you're OK, Granny.'

'Me too, lovey.'

'You'll have to come and stay with us. Won't they, Daddy?'

'Of course.'

'There's no need,' Rosie insisted. 'I'll ring my aunt. She'll squeeze us in.'

'There's no squeezing needed at my place,' Jack said.

'Why, do you live in Buckingham Palace these days?' Rosie remembered the two-up two-down cottage where they started, and ended, their married life.

Jack didn't react to her sharp response. Rosie hated to cede control. That was one reason why marriage came hard to her although he was far from being a domineering man.

He'd always admired the strength inherent in most women and celebrated it every day with his strong-willed daughter. But he completely got that the last thing his ex-wife wanted tonight was any level of reliance on him again.

'It's late and you're cold and tired.' He quietly pointed out the obvious. 'It'll take your family a good half hour to get here.'

'I've got a rental car. Transport isn't an issue.'

'No, but exhaustion and shock are,' Jack insisted. 'You aren't fit to drive. I'll run you back over here to pick the car up tomorrow but meanwhile we'll have you back to St Wenn in about ten minutes for a good hot shower and a strong cup of tea.' Jack winked at Maggie. 'We'll even whip up a strong cup of coffee for our American lady.'

The relief in his former mother-in-law's weary eyes told him the argument worked where she was concerned so he refocused on Rosie.

With no make-up, her hair ruffled and wearing pale blue flowery pyjamas under the emergency blanket she looked little older than the girl he first fell in love with.

'In case you're interested, I don't live in Elm Terrace anymore. Tregony House has plenty of space.'

'Wow — did you win the lottery or something?'

A whoosh of heat lit up his neck and face.

'I . . . '

'Daddy worked hard to make something of himself.' Lisa's fierce defence touched him. 'And all with me under his feet.'

'You were never . . . '

'Don't put yourself down.' She turned her challenging stare on Rosie. 'He gave up school to work in a factory when you got married.'

'I know, I didn't . . . '

'But he went back and trained as a paralegal before becoming a qualified family mediator. Daddy owns a very successful business with about ten other counsellors working for him.'

'That's enough for now, sweetheart. Your grandmother needs her bed.' Jack skipped over any mention of Rosie. 'My car's over there.' He encouraged Lisa and Gino to take care of Maggie and cautiously slipped his arm around his ex-wife's slender shoulders. 'You OK?'

'Ask me again in the morning.'

★ ★ ★

If anyone had told Rosie when she booked a ticket to London that she'd end up sleeping under the same roof as her ex-husband again she'd have labelled them insane.

Now she found herself in Tregony House, the elegant Georgian building they pushed Lisa past in her pram and created dream scenarios of living there one day.

'It's more beautiful than I imagined.' She gazed around the long, wide hall with its pale green walls and perfect off-white moulding and ornate plaster-work ceiling. 'Your decorator did an amazing job, or is Lisa into this kind of thing? It takes a keen eye to modernise without spoiling the traditional style.' Jack's sheepish look returned to amuse Rosie. What did she say to bring that on?

It was still barely seven o'clock but any further sleep had eluded her when she woke up in a strange bedroom.

The sight of a pair of jeans and warm red jumper borrowed from Lisa waiting for her on the chair brought back the horrors of the night before. The few clothes she grabbed when making their hasty exit from the hotel reeked of smoke and weren't fit to wear.

'One Christmas I received an invitation to come here for drinks because I'd done some work for Christian Harold.'

Jack straightened one of the ribbon-back chairs set either side of the front door. 'Everything about this place intrigued me and I started to read up on the era, visited a lot of other houses and . . . '

'Waited?'

'The family had financial problems at the time and I . . . '

'Stepped in to save the day.' Before Rosie could apologise for the unintentional bitterness he reached for her right hand, rubbing his long fingers over her skin in a way that brought back too many memories.

'Still so prickly. Doesn't it get tiring?'

Tears flooded her eyes and she blinked them away to plaster on a smile.

'I thought you weren't supposed to counsel people you're . . . close to?'

Jack gave her a lingering look. She drew in a steadying breath and gathered her see-sawing emotions.

'How about some breakfast?'

'Just coffee for me, please. I haven't

eaten breakfast in years.'

'Never would've guessed.' His appraising gaze swept over her. 'Was this smart, sophisticated Rosalind created to escape everyday Rosie?'

When she didn't immediately answer Jack's brief shoulder shrug said what they both were far too aware of. The past follows wherever people go. This week was living proof.

She'd unwillingly been thrust face to face with her own ghosts after burying them with varying degrees of success for over twenty years.

'I'll call Pam in a minute and we should be out of your hair before lunch. Today will be crazy for you with all the last-minute wedding bits and pieces to organise. We're the last thing you need to worry over.'

Jack stepped closer and his eyes deepened to the intriguing shade of midnight blue resonant in her dreams. Wearing his coat last night with its familiar warm, clean scent felt like having his arms wrapped around her.

Now a drift of the same subtle aroma came her way again. Instinctively, she lifted her hand to his unshaven cheek and rubbed a finger over the soft dark stubble.

'I've never stopped worrying about you,' he said softly.

'Oh, Jack.'

'Daddy, there's some terrible news. You won't believe it!' Lisa pushed Rosie away and flung herself at her father, her eyes wide with panic.

An Inevitable Kiss

Jack clung on to his hysterical daughter and struggled to pick out the occasional clear word between her loud gulping sobs. All he caught was rats, closed and cancelled.

'Calm down, sweetie. I can't help if you don't explain the problem calmly.'

'No-one can help. It's a disaster.'

'Lisa Margaret, get a hold of yourself,' Rosie snapped. 'Kitto women have more gumption than this.'

'You didn't.'

'You're not me. You're better.' The declaration shut Lisa up. 'Unless of course something awful happened to Gino . . .'

'Don't be ridiculous. I'd hardly be . . . oh you're clever.'

Jack stifled a laugh as his daughter cottoned on to her mother's devious comment.

'I'm simply pointing out the obvious.

You'll still get married tomorrow to the man you love — no matter what.'

'Can you believe they found rats in the kitchen at the Rashleigh Grange?' Lisa shuddered. 'The health inspectors threw out all the food.' Her lip wobbled. 'Including our five-tier Italian cream wedding cake.'

A trickle of panic coursed through Jack.

'Can you still use the venue?' Rosie asked.

'No, they found more evidence of rats in the dining-room and closed the whole building.' She glared at her mother. 'Did you remember to pack your magic wand? You solve wedding problems for a living so here's your chance to show me how good you are.' Jack sensed more behind the challenge than a re-imagined reception.

'Look around you.'

'What for?'

'You have a stunning house at your disposal.'

'Oh, right and what are we going to

do for food? Fish and chips from the chippy? Tell our guests to bring a picnic lunch and sit on the floor?'

Rosie grinned.

'You forget I'm friends with the award-winning chef at the Old Goose.'

Lisa's scathing snort made her scepticism clear and Jack rushed to intercede before the confrontation degenerated any further.

'It's very short notice. I can't think . . . '

'I can. Will you at least let me ask Bruno?' The softer pleading tone made his daughter stop shaking her head and stare at her mother.

'Are you serious?'

'What's the worst he can say?' Rosie held up one hand. 'As far as I can tell we've nothing to lose.'

'Well I think it's an amazing idea.' Jack latched on to the suggestion, mainly because he couldn't come up with a viable alternative.

'You would. Ever since she turned up you've been all soppy and weird.'

Now wasn't the time to follow up that particular observation. After he got his daughter happily married to the man of her dreams he'd think it through and consider how true it might be.

'Do you want this sorted out, Lisa, or don't you?'

'Of course, but . . . '

'Then how about being grateful for any help you're offered because Mrs Wheal's shop can't bake that many pasties in time and my cooking skills don't stretch to wedding reception fare, we both know that.' Lisa sagged in front of his eyes. 'Sorry, love, I don't mean to be harsh . . . '

'Yes, you did — but I needed it.' She wrapped her arms around his neck and smacked a big kiss on his cheek. 'You're the best.'

'I'll go upstairs where it's quiet and give Bruno a call,' Rosie murmured.

'Thank you.' Two spots of heat coloured Lisa's cheeks. 'I'm grateful. Really.'

'I'm happy to help. I've failed you all your life but if I can sort this for you . . . ' Rosie bit her lip, swung away from them and took off up the stairs at record speed.

'Oh, Daddy, I feel awful for being so mean.' Lisa blinked back tears.

'Forget it now. We've far too much to do. After the honeymoon you can sort things out with your mother.' How that would work out he couldn't quite imagine but for the moment he'd follow his own recommendation and put the thought away until later.

'My suggestion is that you contact Gino and your bridesmaids plus any other friends who might help and get them over here as soon as possible. I'll ring a few people and call in some favours. We've got a wedding reception to organise.'

*   *   *

Lisa needed her. Her. The incredible idea flooded Rosie's veins with a huge surge of adrenaline. OK, so it was her problem-solving skills that were needed but she'd take what she could get. If it cracked open the door to re-establishing a relationship with her only child she'd claw her way to the top of Mount Everest on her knees.

Get real, Rosalind, she chided herself. Do you honestly believe organising food for a few wedding guests will wipe out years of neglect? She'd been called many things in her time but dumb wasn't one of them.

'Realistic' was Crispin's favourite term for her, expressed with a touch of dismay as though it wasn't human to be so cold and practical.

Her business partner didn't understand the danger of loving too deeply. The moment the doctor placed Lisa in her arms she tumbled head first into a complete all-encompassing love that terrified her.

On the other hand Jack settled into fatherhood as though he'd been doing it all his life and she couldn't express her fears, convinced he wouldn't understand the panic keeping her awake all night and all day until she resembled an exhausted zombie.

Nothing appeared to faze him. The endless hours when Lisa cried and couldn't be comforted. The uncertainty of wondering if they'd have any money left in the bank by pay day. Now she suspected she wasn't being fair — he'd no doubt worried, too, but with her unpredictable moods dared not express his fears.

These days she'd probably be diagnosed with post-natal depression instead of being labelled nothing more than another teenage mother who couldn't cope.

Rosie shook her head. Dredging all this up achieved nothing. She pulled out her phone and tracked down Bruno's number. Time to put super-efficient persuasive Rosalind back into action.

Ten minutes later she ended the call and a broad smile lit up her face from ear to ear. The promise of top billing for the Old Goose on her planned new business expansion won him over — along with the undeniable pleasure of besting one of Cornwall's premier hotels. Publicity was a powerful motivator.

'Hello, love, is it really eight o'clock already?' Her mother stood in the doorway of their shared bathroom wearing a pair of Jack's sweatpants rolled up at the ankles and a baggy grey jumper.

'Don't say it.' Maggie plucked at the too long sleeves. 'I'm some grateful for having them, but . . . '

'We'll get you something that fits later.'

'It's a nice place this. Jack's done all right for himself.'

'He has, Mum.' Was it mean to resent her mother's enthusiasm? Maggie wouldn't rave over her fashionable new apartment in trendy downtown Nashville the same way. Part home and part business setting, she cultivated new clients there for an initial meeting to reinforce her forward looking image. 'Did you sleep OK?'

'Wonderful. I'd happily take the bed home with me.'

Her mother's relaxed smile brought tears to Rosie's eyes. This was the upbeat Maggie of her childhood before her father's long illness and subsequent death took its toll.

'There's something about this place. Do you feel it?'

Oh, she did. Infused with Jack's good taste the house basked in a warm glow that reached beyond paint colours and comfortable beds. It reflected everything good about him. Solid. Calm. But with a flair that showed itself in unexpected touches like an African giraffe carving nestled between a pair of antique botanical prints and the vivid orange silk cushions providing a pop of life on a faded floral sofa.

'Sorry, Rosie. I'm being thoughtless.'

'In what way?'

'I dragged you to Cornwall in the

first place but never expected to end up here. It's got to be hard on you.' Thankfully it wasn't phrased as a question. 'Is there a cup of tea going downstairs?'

'Of course. Wouldn't it be against English law otherwise?' Rosie laughed. 'Now there's a problem with the wedding reception.' She launched into a retelling of the rat story.

'Oh my goodness — that's awful! The poor love.'

For some unfathomable reason the idea of explaining her own role stuck in her throat but there wasn't any use trying to hide it so she forced it out.

'Once I've got Lisa and her friends on the right track sorting out chairs, tables and decorations I'm heading over to the Old Goose. Do you want to stay here or we can call Pam or Aunt Viv to come pick you up if you prefer?'

'I'm sure they can use another pair of hands here.' Her mother's determined streak reasserted itself. 'It's good of you.'

'Good?' Rosie's cheeks flamed. 'She's my daughter. Anyway, let's go and find you a restorative cuppa.'

★   ★   ★

Watching full-on Rosalind giving succinct instructions and firm deadlines made Jack thoughtful. If she never left St Wenn would she still have evolved into this confident, capable woman? He wanted to believe he'd have encouraged her to expand her horizons beyond being his wife and Lisa's mother but couldn't be certain.

'Are you paying attention, Jack? Your task is to count how many chairs you've got scattered around this place and find extras to top it up to at least seventy. I suggest trying the church or community centre. Small tables are essential, too, although the sit-down dinner idea's been abandoned so it'll all be finger food people can eat standing up if necessary.'

'No problem.'

'I need a lift back to Fowey to pick up our car then I'll pop over to see Bruno and you can run back here and get busy.'

'Of course.' Jack's swift agreement made Rosie's eyes gleam and he risked a cheeky wink. Sharing the same sense of humour was something he'd never enjoyed with any other woman. 'I'll throw on a coat and grab my keys. Meet you outside in five minutes.'

Weddings, and the run up to them, were emotional occasions. Keep that to the forefront of your mind, Jack told himself. Do not allow your growing admiration, or stronger, for this new amped-up version of Rosie to gain a foothold.

The mental talking to worked — until she stepped out of the house with her smooth hair swept to one side and generous mouth turned glossy with something deep red and tempting.

'Ready?' Her lips turned at the corners in the familiar secretive smile she tied him up in knots with all those years ago. 'We're doing this for Lisa.' In other words — don't read too much into it.

'Warning duly noted.' Jack received a quizzical glance in return. 'Your carriage awaits, milady.' He opened the car door and startled as she laid her fingers over his hand, sending up a light lemony drift of scent. 'You're wearing Lisa's perfume.'

'I borrowed it, along with everything else. Is it too young for me?' Rosie's low husky laughter skittered over his skin, heating it on contact and tossing logic out of the window.

'Keep asking for compliments and . . . '

'And what, Jack?'

'This is inevitable,' He lowered his mouth to meet her teasing lips and with a soft sweep brushed across, eliciting a throaty gasp from Rosie and triggering a shiver of pleasure all the way to his feet. Somehow he halted the kiss and slid his hands up to cup her face, soaking in the flare of her smoky, expressive eyes.

'I asked for that.'

The uncontrollable tremor running through her words thrilled Jack.

'We both did.'

'We shouldn't do it again.'

'Not ever?'

'We've got a wedding to get off the ground.'

'And after?' he whispered against her silky hair, running his fingers through the layered strands.

'After is up for negotiation.' Rosie lowered her gaze, filtering her expression through a curve of long dark eyelashes. Absurdly it crossed his mind that she must dye those too. In the old days she always complained how pale and straight they were.

'I'm a trained mediator.'

'So you are. Do you succeed with all your clients?'

'If they want resolution badly enough, I do.' Let her read into that as much or as little as she chose. 'Now we should get going. I assume Bruno is expecting you?' By the deepening flush of heat creeping up her elegant neck Jack's abrupt return to normal conversation disconcerted her.

'He is.' Rosie climbed into the car, tucking his daughter's borrowed black raincoat in around her legs. With both hands grasped on her lap and a fixed stare out of the window she made her position as nothing more than a fellow wedding planner perfectly clear.

He'd honour it. For now.

A Broken Promise

After is up for negotiation? Was she out of her mind? Rosie pushed Jack's kiss to the recesses of her brain and concentrated on Bruno.

'Given the time constraint everything must be simple but all made from fresh local produce because I do not compromise there.' He ticked the suggestions off on his fingers. 'Plus we introduce a touch of Italian flair to suit the groom's family. Again that is who I am.' Bruno cocked his head to one side. 'Do you need details or do you trust me?'

Offending him wasn't on her agenda but she suspected her daughter might insist on more in the way of specifics.

'I trust you absolutely because I'm familiar with your stellar reputation.' Buttering up people was usually Crispin's job.

'But?'

'The poor bride is a touch shell-shocked today. She needs reassurance and . . .'

'My indecisive answer might not suffice?' The chef's broad smile relaxed her.

'Do you mind?'

'You are a clever woman.'

'I'll take that as a compliment.'

He lowered his head in a gesture of mock-subservience.

'Exactly how it was intended, dear lady.' Bruno's exuberant laughter ran around the deserted restaurant. With a flourish he produced a printed menu, thrusting it in her hands with another playful smile. 'I am sorry — I like to tease sometimes. My staff is used to it.'

Rosie's mouth watered as she scanned the list.

'I cannot replicate their original menu but I hope the difference will become a bonus. I mixed Italian and Cornish favourites exactly as the new couple are doing with their life together.'

Again she blinked back tears. For an unemotional woman — or at least one who'd trained herself to be so — she'd cried a lot over the last week.

'You have time to make all this?' From her experience miniature hand-held foods were fiddly and her saviour had an award-winning restaurant to run.

'What do you think interns are for?' Bruno chuckled. 'They come to learn from me and last-minute orders and time management are a crucial part of their education. So is getting shouted at if they don't move fast enough. I will send Liam to keep them in order. He is my right-hand man.'

'And your crew will bring everything to St Wenn, set-up, serve and clear away afterwards?'

'Of course.' A frown creased his forehead. 'Do you need us to run a bar as well?'

'Is it too much?'

'Yes, but we will do it anyway.' The dramatic way he tossed his hands in the air held echoes of the half-Italian mother he'd spoken fondly of. His pragmatic side no doubt came from his down-to-earth father, a retired Cornish fisherman. 'Simple again. Prosecco. White or red wine and soft drinks.'

'I hardly dare to ask . . . '

'Will this work?' Bruno took another sheet of paper off the table and grinned. 'It's a cannoli tower.' Tiers of stunning cream-filled cannoli with the ends dipped in crushed pistachios stood on a gold platter decorated with ivory and pistachio green bows echoing Lisa's wedding colours. 'There is no time to recreate the original cake and this way your lovely daughter may not compare the two as harshly.'

'I can't thank you enough.' A rasp of emotion tore at her voice. 'That's not the fellow wedding professional talking but a mother.' She stumbled over calling herself that but couldn't bare her soul to this almost-stranger no matter how kind he'd been.

'Will you allow me to take you out to dinner on Sunday evening?' He asked.

'Dinner?' Rosie repeated. The chef's ruddy skin darkened and he gave a very Mediterranean shrug. Crispin complained she metaphorically closed her eyes to the dating possibilities around her so for once Rosie made an effort to see Bruno in a different light.

Around her own age and attractive in a world-weary way with his dark hooded eyes and swarthy complexion he was far from unappealing. But he's not Jack.

'I'm not sure if I'll still be around.'

'But if you are?' His gentle persistence wormed under her skin and she found herself agreeing.

'Good.' The satisfaction her response evoked touched Rosie. If something were to come of this wasn't that wiser than stirring things back up with her ex-husband?

'I must go. I'll see your hapless

interns tomorrow morning. The ceremony is at noon which means everyone will be back to the house around one o'clock.'

'My people will do most of the prep work here so an hour or so to set up should be fine.' He leaned in closer, spreading his large hands over her shoulders and kissed her cheeks, European style. 'We will not let you down.'

'I'm sure you won't and I'm extremely grateful.' Rosie nodded. 'Thank you.' She caught a flash of unashamed admiration before his friendly smile slid back into place. What was different about her in Cornwall that two eligible men found her so intriguing? It was not a question Rosie was certain she wanted to answer.

★ ★ ★

Retreating to the only unoccupied space he could think of, Jack munched his pasty in the garden shed.

The house swarmed with people obeying Lisa's instructions. With her initial shock in check his daughter almost appeared to be enjoying herself by marshalling her friends and anyone else foolish enough to come near with quasi-military precision.

Thankfully Gino wasn't the stereotypical Italian and stayed calm under pressure, completely unflustered by his bride-to-be transforming into a martinet.

The bridesmaids were busy hanging garlands originally meant for the hotel from every conceivable spot. At least here his chances of being wrapped in cream and green ribbons diminished greatly.

'I guessed I'd find you here.' Rosie poked her head around the door. 'You always hid out among the tools when I got on your nerves.' She stepped over a rake and perched on the bag of compost next to him. 'Any chance of sharing your pasty with me?'

'Good grief, woman — you've been in America too long.' Jack laughed. 'No self-respecting Cornishman shares his pasty. There are plenty more in the kitchen, so help yourself. Feeding and watering everyone was my allotted task once I'd rounded up the tables and chairs.' He reached the last corner of pastry. 'There you go. I'm in a generous mood today.'

She snatched it away and popped it in her mouth.

'That's the best bit. I'd forgotten.'

Jack leaned across to sweep a crumb off her lip but didn't rush to shift his hand away, rubbing his thumb over her warm cheek.

'You promised.'

'This isn't a kiss. Surely you haven't forgotten what one of those is so quickly. I must be slipping.'

'Slipping? That's far from the problem — trust me.' Rosie shifted away. Tidying a strand of hair back from her face she treated him to a stern glare. 'I've two pieces of good news I thought you might be interested in hearing.'

'I am,' Jack protested but she rolled her eyes. 'I've had a lot on my mind.' Including you, he added silently.

'First I stopped by the Heron's Nest because I had to see Demelza after she'd been so kind to us. You were right that the damage looked worse than it turned out to be. It'll be tricky to repair and of course some things are irreplaceable but Demelza hopes they'll be able to re-open later this year. I promised her a publicity boost on the Wedding Wishes site once they're up and running again.'

'That's great.'

'I thought you might also be interested in hearing how I got on at the Old Goose.'

'I'm sure you were successful. Tell me everything.'

She rushed though a detailed explanation of the whole reception food saga and ended with a triumphant grin by describing the cannoli cake.

'You're amazing.' For two pins he'd

wrap Rosie in an all-encompassing hug and plant a loud smacking kiss on her mouth. Out of gratitude. Nothing more. 'Of course I always knew that.'

'Did you?' The low whispered question settled between them. 'Did you really?'

Jack's throat closed. How honest should he be?

'Daddy, you can't hide out here any longer.' Lisa burst in. 'We need . . . ' Her sharp glance shot between him and Rosie. 'When did you get back? Didn't it occur to you I might be interested in knowing if we have food arranged for tomorrow or if I need to stay up all night making sandwiches?'

'I'm sorry, I . . . '

'Your mother's worked miracles.' Jack intervened. They didn't need another emotional set-to. 'She was kind enough to track me down so we could share the good news with you together.' Lisa's sceptical gaze swept over him.

'Meet me in the kitchen.' Lisa swept

out without another word.

Rosie cracked first and erupted into raucous laughter followed right behind by him. This time he didn't resist the urge to hug her.

'Oh Jack,' she spluttered, 'that reminds me of . . . '

'When your mum caught us kissing in your front room instead of studying for our exams.'

'Like this you mean?' Jack cupped the back of her head and drew them into a gentle searching kiss before forcing himself to let go. 'Our daughter's waiting for us.'

'We aren't an 'us' any more.'

'We could be.'

Shock darkened Rosie's eyes and she jumped to her feet, glaring at him.

'The past is the past, Jack. I'm leaving tomorrow evening once everything is cleaned up here.'

'Fair enough.' He'd let his actions speak for him. In the night she'd remember his kiss and then they'd see who could walk out again.

Ill-chosen Words

Please don't cry. I can't bear it, Rosie silently pleaded, torn up by the tears welling in Lisa's big grey eyes.

'Don't you like the menu?'

'No, I definitely don't.'

A vague awareness of Jack caressing her shoulder in a comforting squeeze seeped through and Rosie couldn't find the strength to push him away.

'Because I absolutely love it. It's perfect.'

'Really? You're not saying that to . . . '

'That's not my style.' A brilliant smile lit up her face. 'I'm like you that way — according to Dad.'

'Oh.' Did that mean they'd discussed her? She'd no idea why that took her by surprise.

'Look at this, Gino.' Lisa thrust the menu at her fiancé, who took it with a sideways wink at Rosie. 'Italian antipasto on skewers. Bruschetta and mini pizzas. Grilled garlic shrimp. Bacon-wrapped asparagus.' She beamed at Jack. 'And Daddy, for you and the Cornish brigade there are mini baked potatoes, tiny pasties and cheeseburger sliders. All perfectly recognisable.'

'Anybody would think I'm ninety and never set foot over the Tamar Bridge.' Jack's playful protest made it clear anything pleasing his daughter was fine with him, insults included.

'By the way — where's my mother?' Rosie asked.

'Oh, we sent her off with Granny Eliza. They've gone shopping in Truro. She particularly needed something for the wedding,' Lisa explained and Rosie's heart leapt.

'Wedding? We weren't planning . . . '

'Of course you're coming.'

'That's not a good idea. It'll cause a lot of upset. People will talk and . . . '

'I don't care.'

How to wriggle out of this without

upsetting her precious daughter? Lisa had no real clue about all the problems her father endured after Rosie left. Rosie understood enough from what she'd heard via her mother to take a pretty good guess and wasn't about to stir all that up again.

'How about Granny Maggie slips into the back of the church to see you married and I'll be waiting back here to give a hand with the reception?'

'But you should both sit with the rest of the family at the front.'

Jack met Rosie's eyes in complete understanding.

'Sweetheart. Tomorrow is your day. Yours and Gino's. I'm sure your mum doesn't want any of the attention taken off you both and it will be if she's there in the church — no matter how much you want things to be different. Trust me. Please?'

'Well, all right — but on one condition.'

Right now Rosie would agree to almost anything.

'We're having a small family dinner at the pub after this afternoon's rehearsal and I want you and Grandma Maggie there. Deal or no deal?'

'I don't have anything suitable to wear and there isn't time for me to sneak off to Truro, too.'

'Those fit you just fine.' Lisa nodded at Rosie's borrowed clothes. 'Rifle through my wardrobe and see what you can find.'

Facing down the local gossips in another of her daughter's outfits wouldn't be ideal but she'd been steered into a corner. This smart girl shared her manipulative genes.

'Thanks,' Rosie conceded with as much grace as she could muster and then glanced around the kitchen. 'I'll check it out later but right now there's work to do. When is the florist arriving?'

'She's on the way. Do you mind helping her place the arrangements where you think they'll be best? I'm off to whisk my bridesmaids away for our manicure session and we won't be doing any nail-ruining work after that.'

'I'll be happy to sort that out and we can always move them later if you want.'

'Before she gets swamped again I promised Rosie a pasty.' Jack grasped her elbow. 'The poor woman's fading away. Off you go. Gino, what's on your agenda?'

'If there is nothing you need my help with I will go back to St Austell. More of my family arrived late last night and I have not seen them yet.'

'You go ahead. Everything's under control.' Rosie kept her voice level, determined to sound more confident than she felt.

★   ★   ★

Jack handed Rosie a pasty before grabbing another for himself.

'It's not polite to let you eat alone.'

'They're as good as I remember.' Rosie smiled after the first bite.

'I'd take a guess Mrs Wheal hasn't

143

changed the recipe in fifty years.'

'Why would she?'

'If it ain't broke don't fix it?'

'Was I stupid enough to think that about our marriage?' Every last drop of colour left her face and Jack wished he'd kept his mouth shut. All his professional skills deserted him when faced with the only woman he ever loved.

'Sorry,' he mumbled, 'forget I spoke. That's all in the past and it doesn't matter now. You're great to do all this for Lisa.'

'Great?' Her voice turned shrill. 'She's my daughter. I'd do anything for her. Anything. We both know I messed up big time and nothing can erase that. Arranging a few bits of food and drink is nothing compared to your twenty-five years of being the most awesome father ever. I bet you never let her down.'

'Of course I did and will again.' Jack reached for her hands and tugged her close enough to kiss. But didn't. 'I'm not perfect. No-one is.' Reaching up, he caressed her face. 'Oh Rosie, you were always so hard on yourself. We were teenagers learning to be adults and suddenly responsible for a baby. Of course we were going to mess up. Every parent has regrets but they deal with them and move on.'

'Is that Mr Mediator talking?' Rosie jibed. 'I assume that's either from the chapter on 'The challenges facing young parents' or maybe 'The positive and negative effects of divorce on children'?'

He dropped his hands away.

'I've got work to do. We'll catch up again later.'

'Jack, I . . . '

Part of him ached to challenge her and force Rosie to see the man he'd become rather than the boy she remembered. For 25 years he'd focused on bringing up Lisa the best way he knew how but not perfectly. Far from it. Part of his mediator training involved facing his own failures and hashing them out in group sessions because no-one wants to talk to a holier-than-thou counsellor with no concept of life's grim realities.

The doorbell's impatient jangle saved him.

'I'll get it.' Jack crossed the hall and flung the front door open to Sadie Wickett, grinning at him around a huge vase of lush cream roses. He'd never been so pleased to see the vicar's wife or a bunch of flowers before. 'Come in. Do you want me to take those?'

'I'll see to things here, Jack.' Rosie popped up by his side. 'You carry on. We'll be fine.'

'Oh my, it really is you. I didn't believe the gossip going round.' Sadie's eyes widened and an awkward silence filled the air.

'I completely forgot you two know each other from way back.' Jack wondered when his ex-wife would gather her wits enough to speak. 'Do you need help bringing more flowers in?' Both ignored him and continued to size each other up.

'Yep, here I am in the flesh.' Rosie's brash challenge made him wince. 'I assume 'Down The Garden Path' is you. Love the van.' Bright green and covered with painted flowers of every description the distinctive vehicle couldn't belong to anyone else. Sadie never fell into the traditional vicar's wife mould and was usually kindly called a free spirit — or an ageing hippie by less charitable people.

'Let's carry all the arrangements inside and then work out where to place them,' Rosie suggested.

'Great idea,' Jack agreed. Before Rosie accused him of stepping on her toes he risked a sneaky wink and a flare of heat coloured her cheeks.

'Um, yes. Thanks, Jack.'

He made a quick escape, leaving Rosie to break the ice with Sadie. The kind woman should be an easier target than the more judgemental people she'd come up against later but village memories ran long and deep.

Slipping into professional mode,

Rosie treated Sadie in the same cordial businesslike fashion as any other wedding vendor. They shifted flowers around the house until they were satisfied.

'When Lisa gets back if she wants anything altered I'll get Jack to help.'

'You've changed, Rosie, and I mean that in a good way.'

'I'm not the same chubby uncertain girl, that's for sure.'

'You were only seventeen. We're all works in progress at that stage.' Sadie's nervous laughter broke out. 'I'm still one now.' She patted Rosie's hand and the comforting gesture nearly undid her protective cool front. 'I want you to know that I deeply regret not speaking up for you at the time. William insisted supporting Jack and Lisa was our first priority but that doesn't excuse my behaviour.'

If this woman expected her absolution she'd have a long wait. With the distance of time Rosie saw clearly that a touch of compassion from the people around her might have prevented her making the rash decision to leave. They had rallied around Jack after she went so why couldn't they have done the same for her when she was struggling?

'Lisa's a lovely girl,' Sadie said.

'She is.'

'And Jack's an exceptional father.'

How did Sadie expect her to respond?

'You didn't marry again or . . . '

'No.' Rosie cut off the rest of the question. 'If you don't mind I've a lot more work to do if we're finished here?'

'Of course.' Sadie's kind brown eyes rested on her. 'A word of advice you're totally free to take or leave. If other people reach out to make amends think carefully before you reply.

'Cutting them off might make you feel better in the moment but at the end of the day it might turn into another regret and we all harbour far too many of those.'

A ribbon of fury snaked through Rosie. The utter misery of the first months and years away from her daughter lodged in a bitter corner of her heart.

'Sorry. I didn't mean to offend you.'

'Really? Not how it came across.'

Sadie took a step backwards.

'I thought it might help you . . . '

'To fit into the village again?' Rosie snapped. 'That's one thing I've no desire to do, thank you very much. As soon as tomorrow's celebrations are over with, I'm out of here and I won't make the mistake of coming back again.' She stalked out of the room and slammed the door behind her with Sadie's shouted apology ringing in her ears.

She Has a Nerve!

Something turned Rosie into this cool, distant woman bent on avoiding Jack as if he had a contagious disease. After the wedding rehearsal he tracked her down to share his confused feelings — a mixture of pride at their beautiful daughter entwined with a touch of melancholy but she completely shut him down.

At the time he put her lack of interest down to sadness for missing out on the traditional role as mother of the bride but suspected there was more to it.

'Are you ready, Daddy?' Lisa looped her arm through his. 'Gino's shepherding his lot to the pub and I'm giving the grannies a ride because they've done enough walking for one day. Do you mind bringing my mother along?'

'I'll be happy to, love.' If she'll speak to me, he added silently. 'You go on and we'll join you there.'

Ten minutes later Jack sank into the nearest comfy chair and wondered how to tackle the Rosie problem. Footsteps on the stairs made him turn and he swallowed hard at the sight of his ex-wife. Wearing a pair of Lisa's worn pink pyjamas, barefoot and with her face naked of any make-up she looked sixteen again.

'Would you mind very much telling Lisa I've got a migraine?'

'Yes, I do mind.'

'Oh.' She padded across the room and the drift of her perfume reminded him of peaches warmed in the summer sun. 'Look, I'm really sorry but I made a mistake. I can't do this.'

'You don't have a choice.'

'Of course I do.'

'No, you don't.' Her eyes flared in shock. 'Don't you dare break another promise to our daughter.'

'But Sadie . . .'

'I couldn't care less what Sadie said. You're an adult. Deal with it.'

'Do you talk to your clients this way?'

Frustration pulsed through his blood. Did she still not get it? Better she'd never come back to Cornwall and left them in peace. Rosie stirred up a range of emotions he'd survived without quite well all these years.

'I know it hurts. I get it.'

'No, you really don't.'

The tears welling in her eyes weakened his resolve. It wouldn't take much to wrap his arms around her and . . . Jack glanced at the clock.

'We don't have time for this now. You've got ten minutes to get dressed and then we're leaving.'

'Bully.' She exhaled a heavy sigh and ran back up the stairs.

He rubbed at the nagging headache pulling at his temples and wished the next 24 hours over with.

'I don't want any complaints. It's the best I could manage in ten minutes.'

If the beautiful woman standing in the living-room door was a dream Jack didn't want to wake up.

'You'll do.' His raspy voice gave him away and Rosie's enigmatic smile deepened.

'Don't ever decide to write a book of compliments because it won't sell a single copy.' The soft southern drawl she'd picked up in Nashville became more prominent. 'Lisa's taste in clothes is a little different from mine but hopefully this works.'

A rush of heat made his face burn and Jack struggled to his feet.

'It suits you better.' The simple scoop necked wool dress, in a rich shade of what he'd call dark red, emphasised Rosie's smoky eyes, pale skin and slender curves.

'Don't tell her that.'

'I don't have a death wish,' he scoffed. 'Remember, I somehow survived her teenage years. Treading on eggshells around volatile hormonal girls is one of my specialities.' The light dimmed behind her smile but he couldn't examine every word he spoke. No magic wand could erase the last 25 years. 'We'd better go. Let's ride or we'll be even later.'

'That suits me.' She angled one ankle to show off her towering black heels. 'They were the only suitable pair I found in Lisa's room and they're a size too small which means walking far isn't an option.'

Jack tucked her hand through his arm.

'I'll make sure you don't fall over.'

'Still protecting me?'

His smile faded to nothing.

'It can't make up for the terrible job I did when we were married.'

'Stop beating up on yourself.'

'You should do the same.'

'Get your keys and on the way you can give me a rundown on tonight's cast of characters.'

'We're not done with this conversation.'

'For now we are.'

Jack's piercing blue eyes narrowed but he didn't say a word.

Out in the car she sneaked a glance

155

over at him, still trying to work out how he'd avoided being snatched up since their divorce. He must top the local area's list of eligible men with his rugged good looks, undoubted intelligence, great sense of humour and clear passion for his successful business. Rosie couldn't come up with any obvious negatives.

* ★ *

Wow. Way to silence a crowded public house. Anyone would think the Queen had unexpectedly wandered in, judging by the stunned silence. A low buzz of whispered conversation swirled around them and Rosie couldn't help picking out a few choice phrases.

'Can't believe she's got the nerve. Look at her, all dolled up. Poor old Jack needs his head tested. I bet that lovely girl doesn't want her around.'

Her nerve faltered until Jack took her arm and steered them towards the private back room.

'Sorry about that.'

'Doesn't matter.' Rosie's fake indifference wouldn't fool him but it was the best she could manage. The second he opened the door and Lisa caught sight of them her daughter's broad smile pushed everything else away.

Swept into the noisy chaos she allowed Gino to introduce her to his family and ended up sitting between his brother and sister. In the middle of fielding Maria's endless questions she picked up on Jack's amusement before someone else drew his attention away. Perhaps later they could swap notes.

No. Bad idea. You're in danger of falling under Jack Kitto's spell again and you don't want that. Do you? Back in Nashville her indifference to any interest from potential boyfriends always led them to look elsewhere but now she could admit, if only to herself, that none of her would-be suitors ever lived up to Jack.

As the party started to break up she sought out her mother.

'Are you ready to go?'

'If you don't mind I'm going to walk over to Eliza's house with her. She's going to show me all her photo albums of Lisa.' Maggie's smile faltered. 'Do you want to join us?'

'I don't think so.' The idea of a parade of pictures to rub in all she'd missed didn't appeal. 'I'm pretty tired and ready for bed.' Her mother's disappointment couldn't be hidden and Rosie struggled to appease her. 'You obviously had a successful shopping trip because that dress really suits you. Black and white is always smart.'

'I haven't bought any new clothes in donkey's years.' A touch of heat blossomed on her round cheeks. 'I went a bit mad and bought two. The one I'm wearing tomorrow is a pretty dark green to blend in with Lisa's colours.'

Rosie didn't point out that they weren't properly invited and wouldn't be included in any family pictures.

'I'm sure it's lovely.'

'You're looking smart, too, and by

Jack's smile he obviously agrees.'

'Don't read too much into that.' Rosie was determined to squash her mother's wishful matchmaking before it took root. 'He's in a good mood, that's all.'

'You never were good at seeing what's under your nose. Always too busy looking off in the distance for something new and different.'

Could Maggie be right? In Rosie's work she strove to pin down the next big thing in weddings to stay ahead of the competition but in her personal life? Over the years she changed exercise programmes, diets, and apartments. Rosie saw that as a sign that she wasn't an old fashioned stick-in-the-mud but perhaps it signified a lack of confidence.

Unable to draw her gaze away from Lisa and Gino she blinked back tears as they wrapped each other in a tight embrace and kissed as if no-one else existed.

The suppressed excitement of her own wedding eve flooded back. Because parental approval on both sides was grudging, everything about their nuptials was quiet.

Their simple registry office ceremony was only attended by their immediate families and Rosie's wedding dress, a cheap white polyester gown, was a bargain picked up in the sales. Despite Jack's ill-fitting dark suit and gaudy red tie, in Rosie's eyes he'd never looked more handsome.

'They're good together.' Jack's low whisper made Rosie jump and his warm breath on the back of her neck and tease of his familiar cologne rattled her even further. 'Ready to call it a night?'

The casual way his strong hands spread over her shoulders, intuitive fingers rubbing at the precise spots where her tension settled, deepened the whirlwind of emotions threatening to make her lose all notion of common sense.

'I've got a decent single malt waiting back at the house.'

'I suppose I could force one down.'

Rosie Trethewey, you need your head tested, she thought.

All I Ever Wanted

Somewhere between the pub and now Rosie had touched up her dark, glossy lipstick and in the soft light from the lamps on either side of the sofa her luminous beauty glowed.

'Do you remember our first date?' Jack asked. While trying to pluck up the courage to put his arm around Rosie he dumped buttered popcorn all over her in the back row of the cinema.

'The stains never came out of my white jeans.'

Jack poured their drinks and passed one to her.

'This should blend in with the dress far better.'

'Lisa won't be happy if I mess it up.'

'She's too busy fussing over flowers and tomorrow's weather forecast to care.' He grinned. 'Thirteen degrees Celsius, about fifty-six Fahrenheit, if you're interested. Cloudy with a ten percent chance of a shower.'

'Sit with me.' Rosie patted the seat next to her.

'Is that wise?'

'Oh, Jack.' Her throaty laugh echoed around the room. 'I can control myself if you can.'

'You aren't sixteen.'

A deep flush crept up Rosie's neck and flooded her face as his unspoken thoughts filled the space between them. She made a point of sitting on her hands.

'Is that better?' A twitch of amusement curled her lips and he couldn't help chuckling. 'Kind of makes it impossible to drink my whisky but that's a minor detail.'

Jack perched on the sofa and held his glass up to her mouth.

'I'll share.'

'That's more than you were willing to do with your pasty,' Rosie teased. She sipped the amber liquid, her gaze meeting his over the rim of the glass to send a rush of heat zooming through him that couldn't be blamed on the strong drink. 'You finish it.' She retrieved one hand and pushed the glass towards Jack.

'What are we doing? And don't say drinking together.'

'But it's true.' Now she glanced towards the floor so he couldn't read her expression. 'Partly.' Rosie sighed. 'I thought it'd be smart to hash things out.'

'Why not add 'to get closure on us' and be done with it?'

'Is that a standard mediation phrase?'

The sharp edge to her question brought Jack back to reality. Pretending they could resurrect a long-dead marriage was beyond foolish on his part. Their lives travelled down different paths a long time ago.

'It works.'

'I can't keep apologising.'

'I don't need you to.' Jack shrugged. 'Lisa's another story.'

'Yeah, I know.'

He set down the glass and took a couple of steadying breaths, at least in theory. They failed.

'Kiss me.'

'Why?' Touching his trembling finger to her jaw forced Rosie to glance back up. Big mistake. Despite the many physical differences in the new Rosalind, two crucial things remained the same. The charcoal grey eyes, always so expressive of her unfiltered emotions, brimmed with longing.

His gaze lingered on her generous mouth where a trace of fine lines softened the edges of her lush lips and the added touch of character only made her more beautiful.

'Because of the way you're looking at me.' Husky and low her voice trickled over his skin. 'So, you see, it's all your fault.'

'I can't help it. Never could around you.' Weaving his fingers through her hair, Jack pulled her close.

'Stay.' Rosie's eyes flared in shock. 'I meant stay here in Cornwall after the wedding for a bit longer.' His stammered explanation didn't convey half of what he wanted to express.

'I've got a business to run.'

'Can't your partner manage for another week or so?'

If Jack would stop feathering kisses on her forehead and cheeks with a bewitching sparkle in his deep blue eyes maybe she could think straight.

'Don't you need to get back to work?'

'There's nothing I can't reschedule.' The unspoken words 'for you' resounded in her head. 'You mentioned expanding your wedding services to Europe so wouldn't doing research around here count as work?'

'It might, but . . . ' Breaking her heart a second time over Jack wasn't happening. 'This is skewing things.' Rosie pushed him away and waved her arm around the room, fragrant with roses and eucalyptus. 'All I want is to make peace with you and Lisa.'

'Is it?'

Ignoring Jack's sad tone she managed to nod.

'Mainly for my mum's sake.' Fudging the truth she could do but blatant lies were never her style. 'Mine, too. I'll sleep easier at night knowing you both don't completely hate me.'

'Hate you? Oh, Rosie, I could never hate you.'

'But I walked out and abandoned our daughter. What kind of woman does that?'

He seized her hands.

'A teenage girl suffering from post-natal depression, stuck in a tiny house with a screaming baby and a young husband who didn't know how to help her.' Jack brushed away the tears trickling down her face.

'I've been on a few dates over the years.' He cracked a wry smile. 'Even tried to talk myself into getting serious with one nice lady.'

Jealousy caught Rosie unawares.

'But in the end it wouldn't have been fair to her so I broke it off.' Pressing a soft kiss on Rosie's damp cheek he stared deep into her eyes, making her wish she possessed the strength to look away. 'None of them were you and you're all I ever wanted.'

'I don't know what to say. I'd no idea!' Rosie sighed. 'That's a lie. I did. And it scared me.'

'I scared you?'

'No.' How to explain without sounding crazed? 'My partner, Crispin, says I'm too cold and rational to be human. He's convinced I'm an alien life form.' She struggled to laugh at herself before giving up.

'You felt so much it frightened you?'

'Don't play the counsellor with me. I'm fine the way I am.' The protest rang hollow but she ploughed on. 'I'm happy with my single independent life and awesome business. It's all I need.'

'If you say so.' He jumped up and wandered across the room to stare out of the window into the starry darkness.

'I've got an active social life in Nashville.' A slight exaggeration but

Rosie couldn't stand the waves of sympathy emanating from Jack. 'I simply prefer to be alone at the end of the day.'

'That's all right, then. Personally I don't — but we're all different.'

'I'm off to bed. We've got an early start in the morning.' What kept her feet fixed to the ground instead of running out of the room and upstairs as fast as possible? 'Are you OK?'

'Fine. Don't worry about me.' Jack turned. 'I'll get the car and go pick up your mum. I can picture mine insisting on walking back here with Maggie and then stumbling home in the dark on her own. I admire the fact she doesn't care what people think but . . . '

'She takes it to extremes?'

'You could say that.'

'It's not far. I'll walk over. I'm sorry it didn't occur to me.' Because I'm too wrapped up in sorting out my confused feelings about you, she almost said aloud.

'It's OK. I don't mind and then you

won't get . . . ' Even in the shadows she caught him blush. 'You said they planned to look at pictures and you don't need . . . '

'Any more guilt laid on me?' Rosie scoffed. 'Don't worry. She can't dump more on my head than everyone else has over the years — plus the bucket loads I've heaped on myself at regular intervals.'

'Doesn't it wear you out?'

'I refuse to let it.'

'We could go together.'

'Jack, give up.' Rosie's voice rose. 'For heaven's sake, go upstairs and get some sleep. Lisa doesn't need a haggard father walking her down the aisle tomorrow.'

For all her brave talk, Rosie dreaded the next day. Being an absent mother 4,000 miles away was borderline tolerable but this verged on torture.

To be in the midst of all the wedding plans but not able to play the part of a real mother hurt so badly she thought she might split in two. She should have turned around and walked out that day in the Old Goose to save them all a lot of hassle. Before he could start on her again she turned on her heels and ran out of the house, slamming the front door behind her.

*　*　*

Like mother like daughter. Despite everything, Jack smiled and kept his fingers crossed the door hinges held out. His gaze fell on the antique roll top desk he bought in an auction last year.

Ignoring the logical side of his brain which told him not to be foolish he opened one of the drawers and removed a white leather album. After Rosie left he came across the handful of photographs that were the only concrete reminder of their short-lived marriage and sorted them out. He'd never looked at them since.

He topped up his whisky glass and sank into his favourite chair. The worn dark green velvet and sagging springs didn't match the rest of the room but he didn't care. His parents gave it to them when he and Rosie had no furniture with which to start their married life.

'You're hopeless. Fancy falling asleep in the chair like an old man. My mum's home safely and tucked up in bed. I came down to make myself a coffee. Do you want one?'

'No, thanks.' Jack levered up out of the chair and the book slid off his lap. They almost banged heads bending to pick it up at the same time.

'Are you getting sentimental tonight too and reliving your little girl's life before you hand her over to another man?' Rosie smiled and flipped the book open. 'Oh.' All the colour drained from her skin and he thought she might faint. 'Where on earth did you find these?'

'I've always had them.' He studied her as she slowly turned the pages, biting her lower lip and running her fingers over the photographs.

'Wow, we were so young.'

A question he'd never dared ask before slipped out.

'Why were you so keen to get married? Apart from the fact I'm irresistible.' Jack tried to crack a joke. 'You used to complain I was too serious and said we should date other people then all of a sudden you changed.'

'You'll be mad when I tell you. My cousin Pam kept flaunting her engagement ring around and boasting about her fancy wedding plans.' A flush of embarrassment heated her face. 'I thought it'd be a bit of a laugh to go down the aisle first.'

'A laugh?' He couldn't get his head around the bizarre explanation. 'You married me to get one over on Pam?'

'Not totally. I loved you,' Rosie protested. 'And I knew you loved me. I thought it'd be fun. We'd have been OK . . . '

'If you hadn't slipped up and got pregnant with me?' A white-faced Lisa hovered in the doorway. 'She needs to get out of our house right now.'

'Take it easy, love.' Jack rushed towards his distraught daughter but she held out her hands to prevent him getting any closer. 'Your mum's not going anywhere.'

'It's OK, Jack I'll leave.' Rosie's eyes glittered with unshed tears. 'She's right to call me out. I'm thoughtless and don't know when to keep my mouth shut.' She focused on Lisa.

'If you don't mind I'll still oversee the reception set up tomorrow because Bruno will expect it.'

Jack noticed her trembling hands pressed into her sides and ached to do or say something to make this right.

Mum's the Word

Rosie watched a wordless exchange between the two before Lisa gave a careless shrug.

'Fine. Whatever. Stay. I suppose it's too late to go anywhere else tonight.'

'Thank you.' Rosie couldn't meet Jack's gaze, too ashamed of upsetting their beautiful daughter on the eve of her wedding. Before he could try to stop her Rosie escaped back upstairs and flung herself on the bed, cramming her face in the pillow so no one would hear her sobs.

Jack hit the nail on the head earlier when he guessed she'd be corralled at Eliza's and practically forcefed Lisa's life story in photographs. It'd taken every last ounce of determination she possessed not to break down in front of them but now it all flooded out.

To realise Jack had carried a torch for

her all these years, combined with the memory of his searing kiss did nothing to comfort her because it only emphasised what she'd lost. Or rather they'd lost as a couple and a family.

As her tears dried, Rosie fell into an exhausted sleep and only stirred at a loud banging on her door.

'Are you awake in there?' Jack's irate voice penetrated her consciousness. 'It's nearly ten o'clock and Lisa's a bag of nerves because the caterers have arrived and you're supposed to be sorting it all out but you're nowhere in sight.'

Dragging herself out of bed she cracked open the door, yawning and dragging her fingers through the birds' nest on her head.

'Oh, heavens, I'm . . . '

'Sorry. You always are.' His resigned sigh sliced through her. 'Stupid me. I thought for once you wouldn't let us down.'

'Jack, I must've . . . ' Rosie bit back the rest of her worthless apology. Letting her family down was what she did. 'Give me five minutes and I'll be there.' Now she bitterly regretted forgetting to set an alarm last night but hadn't slept past seven o'clock in decades. She retreated to the bathroom for what her mother would call a 'lick and a promise' wash.

Rosie tugged on black leggings, a black tunic and flat shoes but took a reckless extra 20 seconds to apply a layer of pillar-box red lipstick before bracing herself to face the day.

At Wedding Wishes she specialised in solving her couples' unusual requests and left the on-the-day touchy-feely side of things to Crispin but today there was no getting out of it.

Arranging a newly married couple's speed boat to their waterside reception was a piece of cake compared to soothing a bride's nerves if her candy floss pink roses verged on fuchsia.

'Finally.' Lisa's rolled eyes and dismissive tone said it all when she joined them in the entrance hall. 'Dad doesn't have a clue and I'm supposed to . . . '

'It's OK, I'll take it from here.'

'My hairdresser's on her way. The bridesmaids are getting ready in their own homes and meeting up here . . . ' Lisa glanced at the clock and groaned. 'Oh, heavens, in another hour.'

Rosie hesitated to ask the next question in case Lisa thought she was sticking her nose in where she plainly wasn't wanted.

'Are they going to help you dress?'

'Don't be silly. I've dressed myself since I was five years old.'

Rosie held her tongue. Brides' nervous fingers turned to jelly on wedding days to make zips and buttons insurmountable obstacles.

'No problem. I'd better get busy.'

'Anything I can do?' Jack ventured.

'Get dressed? I assume that's not your wedding gear?' Despite the ragged jogging bottoms and a baggy green jumper Rosie swore she remembered from 25 years ago the sight of her handsome ex-husband still made her heart beat faster.

'Hardly.'

'Off with you then.' She'd concentrate far better without him under her feet. Left alone, Rosie plastered on a smile and headed for the kitchen where five young people in chef's whites stared at her expectantly. Instantly she switched into work mode. This she could do.

* * *

Jack checked his tie in the mirror and mentally pictured how different things should've been today. Rosie would be fussing over them to make sure he and Lisa were dressed properly while they all laughed and shed a few tears together.

Then she'd slip into an elegant mother-of-the-bride outfit topped with an extravagant hat and kiss him before going to the church to wait for them to arrive.

'Daddy, my zip's stuck.' Lisa burst in, her eyes brimming with tears and flung herself at him. 'I'll be walking down the aisle with my bum hanging out if you can't fix it.'

'Calm down, sweetheart. Let me take a look.' Gently turning her around he fiddled with the zipper, able to see the delicate fabric caught in the teeth but afraid to tug too hard in case he made things worse. 'I wonder if . . . '

'No!' Lisa glared back over her shoulder. 'You're not asking my useless mother. Try.'

Jack cautiously wriggled it around but nothing shifted.

'I'm sorry, love but it's not going anywhere and my fingers are too big. How about calling one of your brides-maids?'

'We don't have time for that.' Her colour deepened. 'I suppose you'll have to fetch HER up here.'

When he didn't immediately reply Lisa paled.

'Maybe after what I said last night she won't . . . '

'I'm sure she will.'

180

Defending Rosie came automatically to Jack because after all he'd done it since he was sixteen but this morning he needed to tread with care.

'You want me to put myself in her shoes for a minute and stop being a spoilt cow.'

Not exactly how he'd have phrased it.

'I'll grovel. All right?'

Jack cracked a smile and leaned in to give Lisa a kiss.

'You're a good girl and Gino's a very lucky man. Don't worry, Rosie will sort you out in no time.' Deep down he couldn't give up on the idea of some level of reconciliation between the three of them. If he was honest, he wanted a sight more than reconciliation. 'I'll find her.'

'Thanks, Dad, you're the best.'

Jack ran downstairs and ground to a halt at the sight of multiple stations already set up for food and drink. The savoury smell of baking wafting out from his kitchen made him hungry. He spotted Rosie gazing out the French windows into the garden.

'Everything under control?'

'Of course.' Rosie checked him out and gave an approving nod. 'You're looking good.'

'Thanks but there's a crisis upstairs.'

'Bridal nerves? That's normal.'

Jack shook his head.

'I could cope with that. The zipper's stuck on Lisa's dress. She's panicking and I'm worse than useless.'

'OK . . . ' The long dragged out word spoke volumes. He caught a touch of wary pleasure in Rosie's expression. 'You stay here have a drink or something and leave us girls to it.'

Rosie's stomach churned but she slid on her confident put-your-trust-in-me smile, the one she reserved for her most anxious clients. She grabbed her handbag from the chair and raced up the curving staircase to knock on Lisa's door.

'Oh. It's you.' A tinge of heat played on her daughter's pale cheeks.

Rosie had heard of shock causing the

breath to leave someone's body but never experienced it before this moment. Faced with her beautiful girl transformed into a bride, Rosie struggled to speak.

'Not many women can carry off Maggie Sottero at her most dramatic but you totally rock that dress.' The extravagant tulle ball gown accented with dazzling Swarovski crystals, a delicate satin belt and pearl buttons was the polar opposite of her own simple wedding dress.

'Before I tried it on I thought I wanted something more classic but I'm afraid I couldn't resist.' Lisa's blush deepened. 'Gino's very Italian in some ways and he'll love all the froth and sparkle.'

'Your dad tells me there's a dress emergency.'

'I don't know what I'll do if you can't help me fix this zipper . . .'

'I'll sort it.' Rosie wasn't tactless enough to ask her daughter to trust her. 'Turn around.' The zipper was caught on the surrounding tulle. 'No problem,

I've dealt with far worse than this.'
Rosie pulled a pencil out of her bag.

'What on earth are you doing?'

'It's an old trick but only works with a real graphite pencil.' Rosie rubbed the teeth on both sides of the zipper with the pencil.

'Here we go.' Giving it a gentle wiggle she exhaled with sheer relief as the zipper began to shift. She eased it all the way up before fastening all the miniscule pearl buttons. 'All done.'

'Seriously?'

'Yep.'

'That's incredible.' Lisa's smile wavered. 'I owe you an apology.'

'Me? You certainly don't.'

'The way I spoke to you last night . . . '

'Shush. I could unzip zippers from now until eternity and never make up for abandoning you.'

'Daddy tried to explain, but it's still . . . hard for me to wrap my head around.'

'Maybe when you're back from

honeymoon and settled in Rome
. . . no, forget it.' Normally she fell into
the if-you-don't-ask-you'll-never-know
school of going along but this didn't fall
in that category.

'I'd love you to come and visit us.'
Lisa half-whispered and one of the
cracks in Rosie's heart began to mend.

'Really?'

'Yes, really . . . Mum.'

Tears trickled down Rosie's cheeks.
This was all she'd ever wanted. To hear
her daughter call her again by the name
she'd recklessly given up all rights to.

'Is everything all right?' Jack stuck his
head in around the door and glanced
anxiously at them both.

'Everything's perfect.' Lisa's declaration made him smile before the
overwhelming emotion Rosie couldn't
hide plainly registered.

'Lovely, isn't she?' Now his eyes
welled up.

Rosie nodded.

'I must get back downstairs and
make sure Bruno's people are on task.'

'I really wish you'd come to the ceremony.'

She steeled herself against her daughter's touching plea.

'I can't and you know why. I'll be here when you all get back from the church.' The sound of the chiming doorbell couldn't be more opportune. 'That's probably your bridesmaids. I'll send them up.'

'I'll come too.' Jack grabbed her arm and steered her from the room, wearing the same determined look on his face she'd seen a million times before.

Moving On

'Don't Jack.'

'Don't what?' He ignored Rosie's blistering stare. 'Is there anything wrong with wanting . . . '

'Yes. For a start I've seriously far too much to do to pull off this reception and I meant what I said to Lisa.' Rosie's eyes softened. 'I agreed to talk to you after all this is over.'

'To keep me quiet.' Jack should feel guilty using his counselling skills in his favour but he'd do whatever it took to gain him the sliver of a second chance. 'Tomorrow evening. Have dinner with me. Everyone will have gone.'

'I expect my mother will be ready to get on home by then.' A deep blush heated her cheeks. 'Plus I've already got . . . something planned.'

'A date?' An unwanted surge of jealousy coursed through Jack's veins and he jammed his hands into his pockets.

'Don't do that.'

'What?'

'You'll crease your trousers.'

'I don't care . . . '

'Lisa will.' Rosie silenced him. 'She won't appreciate you showing her up in front of her smart new Italian relatives.'

'Who's the lucky man?' He watched the wheels turn as she caught up with his question.

'Bruno from the Old Goose but it's not a date. Not really. At least it isn't as far as I'm concerned.'

Jack would bet anything it certainly was in the chef's eyes.

'Fine, then it'll have to be tonight before you run off again.'

'Oh, will it?'

'Is that a problem?'

'I suppose not.'

Not the last word in enthusiasm but he'd take what he could get and work around it.

'I'm going to check on the cars. I'll

leave you to whatever it is you're doing.' Jack couldn't walk away without saying one more thing. 'You and Lisa seemed different together just now. Was it simply happiness over an unstuck zipper or something more?'

'She asked me to visit them in Rome.' Rosie stared down at her feet before lifting her head to meet his gaze again. 'It's all down to you.'

'I didn't do anything.'

'Oh, Jack. You could've bad-mouthed me to Lisa all these years but you never did.' The tiny smile curving Rosie's soft mouth making him ache to kiss her again. 'Go on.' She gave him a gentle push. 'It's your task to get our beautiful daughter safely married . . . for both of us.' The rasp of her broken voice almost finished him off but Jack managed a sharp nod.

Downstairs he was faced with a blur of laughing girls in a swirl of green frothy dresses. Katie, Vicky and Rach, Lisa's best friends since they started school together at five years old.

They were officially grown up and with successful, responsible careers — a doctor, accountant and estate agent — but he still pictured them running around the house with skinned knees, missing teeth and illicitly applied make-up.

'Well, Uncle Jack, aren't you the handsome one today?' Vicky slipped her arm through his and burst into a trill of laughter. 'Don't you think we've cleaned up well too?' She wagged her finger. 'No tears allowed — at least not until you hand Lisa over to that impossibly handsome Italian. Find our car and pack us off to the church.'

⋆ ⋆ ⋆

For a moment the house settled into something close to silence apart from faint voices drifting in from the kitchen where Bruno's cheerful workers were taking a well-earned break. Rosie had sent her mother off with a practised smile and ordered her to remember every detail of the service to share later.

She stopped in the middle of tweaking a flower arrangement and wandered out into the hall. The moment she opened the front door and heard the church bells ringing a wash of emotion threatened to swamp her.

A vivid picture of the scene now taking place at the church filled her head. The last few guests would be hurrying in to find their seats.

She could imagine Gino standing nervously at the front of the church with his best man and the vicar giving him encouragement.

The three bridesmaids would be hovering outside fiddling with each other's hair and joking about which one of them would be next up the aisle.

Rosie had peeked out of an upstairs window to watch Lisa and Jack climb into a gleaming dark green Rolls-Royce fluttering with cream silk ribbons. No rain. Cornwall had turned on a perfect soft mid-February day complete with early daffodils blooming for her girl.

Was Jack saying a few calming words to Lisa now? Maybe simply telling her how proud he was and how much he loved her.

'Ms Trethewey, we need your opinion on whether to put a few chairs outside for the inevitable smokers. Uh . . . Ms Trethewey, are you all right?'

Rosie glanced back over her shoulder to find one of Bruno's protégées giving her a worried frown.

'I'm sorry, did you say something?' Rosie asked. The girl patiently repeated herself. 'That's a good idea. I'll be right with you.'

After situating half a dozen chairs at the far edge of the back patio, Rosie took a moment to glance around and allowed herself a mental pat on the back. No-one would guess holding the reception here wasn't Lisa and Gino's original intention.

Rosie had spent hours polishing Jack's beautiful antiques and along with the stunning flowers and appetising aroma of good food people should feel welcome the minute they stepped inside.

The bells started to ring again signifying the end of the service and Rosie raced back upstairs to change out of her work clothes and freshen up her hair and make-up.

Her fingers shook sliding up the zipper of the sapphire blue dress she'd borrowed from Lisa, a trifle shorter than she usually wore and more close-fitting but it would serve the purpose. She intended to stay as unobtrusive as possible.

Get through the next few hours and then you can go on a not-date with the ex-husband you're still in love with, she told herself.

She slipped back into the kitchen seconds before Jack's voice boomed out.

'Wherever you're hiding, Rosie, come out.'

Smoothing down her dress she picked up a jug of water and moved towards the door as he flung it open.

'Oh, you're back.'

'As if you didn't know.'

The admonition made her cheeks burn.

'Put that down and come with me.'

'Don't boss me around, Jack Kitto.'

'Mum, where are you?' The sound of Lisa's voice shut them up.

'Do it for her.'

Rosie nodded.

'Sorry, it's just . . . hard.' Before he could start on her again she rushed on. 'I know I deserve hard. I'm not stupid.'

'Come on.' Jack grabbed the jug and plonked it on the table. 'We'll talk later and yes — that's a promise.' Slipping his arm around her waist as though he absolutely still had the right to do so he flashed a mischievous smile when she stiffened against him. 'You make a pretty hot mother-of-the-bride in my opinion.'

'It's Lisa's dress.'

His dark blue eyes lit up.

'No offence to the dress but it's the woman inside who wins me over. You'd be beautiful wearing a plastic bag.'

What to say to such a man? Rosie might as well be sixteen again, tongue-tied and helpless against Jack's easy charm.

'Take me to meet the brand new Mr and Mrs Gino Rossi.'

Seeing the new glossy version of his first love disconcerted sent a surge of hope through Jack. Time was running out to persuade her to give them another chance. After they kissed again for the first time in 25 years he'd admitted to himself that whatever it took he'd fight to win Rosie back.

'Willingly.' Jack opened the kitchen door. 'I found her.'

'You certainly did.'

Lisa's ambiguous comment made him blush. Being the two of them on their own for so long they understood each other better than most fathers and daughters. At the moment he couldn't be sure how she felt about his obvious admiration for the woman who'd abandoned them both.

'Don't I get a hug, Mum?'

Rosie froze until he gave her a gentle push and Jack exchanged a satisfied smile with Gino as the two women embraced. Only last week that would've seemed an impossibility.

'I want you to join us and greet our guests.'

'I can't . . . '

'You can and will.' Lisa's firm order made him smile. Talk about the apple not falling far from the tree.

'It'll be all right.' Jack's effort to reassure Rosie earned him a resigned shrug. 'Come on.' He tucked her arm through his and they stood in place as the first people started to arrive. Tension radiated through her and he did his best to brush off several pointed questions.

'Everyone should be here which means it's time to test the food. I'm starving,' Lisa declared. 'I was too nervous to eat any breakfast.'

'I cannot have my beautiful new wife fading away.' Gino laughed and swept her off, leaving Jack and Rosie alone.

'I ought to . . . '

'In a minute.' Jack wrapped his arms around her, relishing the complete rightness of holding her again. 'You smell wonderful. It's different from Lisa's perfume that you borrowed.'

'I managed to buy a bottle of my regular perfume while I was out.'

'It's similar to the one you used to wear years ago but . . . '

'A lot more expensive. I've moved on in that department and many other ways, Jack.'

'Too far?'

'For what?'

'To find your way back to me . . . to us.'

Rosie touched her fingers to his mouth.

'Shush. This is talk for tonight. Right now you need to drink champagne and toast our lovely daughter and her handsome husband.'

'I will. After this.' Jack caught her tighter to him and dragged them into a long, deep kiss, the remembered taste of her shocking him with its intensity.

Pulling away before he said or did something out of place he rested his hand against her cheek.

'Later.' He turned and walked away, sensing Rosie watching and hoping the same buzz of anticipation disturbed her, too.

Heartfelt Praise

'How are you holding up, love?' Maggie cornered Rosie over by the temporary bar, set up on one side of the French doors.

'You know how hospitals always quote 'as well as can be expected' — well, that's me. It's OK, I'll get through it. Was the ceremony beautiful?' Rosie asked the question to take attention away from herself.

She'd experienced a mixture of open disdain and curiosity from people finding her a part of the receiving line. There was no getting away from her actions of 25 years ago and all most guests saw was a neglectful mother worming her way back into her daughter's special day and poor Jack being taken in again.

'Yes.' Her mother's eyes welled with tears. 'I missed you and your father but

I'm so glad we came.'

'So am I.' The chance to see her daughter as a bride and help in a small way to make Lisa's wedding go smoothly far outweighed the pain Rosie had become accustomed to carrying around. 'I expect you'll be ready to go home tomorrow?'

'Tomorrow? We can if you want, but Eliza asked if we'd join them for lunch at the Red Lion. I bet it's years since you had a good Sunday roast with all the trimmings.'

Rosie had fought hard to attain a decent figure and it wouldn't remain that way with regular doses of Yorkshire pudding and thick slabs of roast beef.

'Aren't you having dinner with that chef chap in the evening?' her mum asked.

'I'm considering cancelling.'

'He seemed nice to me.'

In other words you're forty-three and single.

'He's a good-looking professional man. What's the problem?'

'He is. Very nice indeed.'

'But he's not Jack.'

Rosie's cheeks flamed.

'Oh, lovey, I've seen the way you two look at each other when you think no-one's paying attention. Are you planning to give him another chance?'

'Me give him another chance? Have you forgotten who left whom? Jack wants to take me out for dinner tonight and have a proper talk. I agreed because I thought I could but now I think it's a ridiculous idea.' She seized a glass of champagne off the bar and knocked it back in one gulp.

'I must check everything's on track in the kitchen. It's nearly time for the toasts and cake cutting.'

'Love is never ridiculous.' Maggie grasped Rosie's hand, stopping her from leaving. 'Crazy, maybe, but not ridiculous.'

The assertion stopped her dead.

'Your father could be a challenging man to live with but I'd give anything for another day with him. Without him there's no . . . colour.' A single tear snaked down her cheek.

No colour. That summed up what was wrong with Rosie's own existence. Weeks, months and years slipped away unnoticed. Coming back to Cornwall and facing her family again had brought Rosie up short in a multitude of ways.

'Oh, Mum.' Rosie wrapped her arms around her mother. 'I'll go out with Jack and we can stay on here until Monday if it makes you happy. After that I've really got to be getting back.'

The hint of a satisfied smile told her she'd walked into her mother's web as willingly as an oblivious fly.

★   ★   ★

Although Jack made his way around the house chatting to everyone he never lost track of Rosie who was carefully staying in the background.

She skirted around the outside of the room carrying trays of glasses or extra food rather than make her way through clusters of guests and be forced to talk.

Until one of his aunts shook her head and made a pointed comment earlier he hadn't registered the extent of the hard situation he'd forced Rosie into.

'I thought Eliza must've finally lost her marbles when she claimed you'd turned up again. Jack's done a good job by our Lisa. I suppose you'll be off back to America after this?'

Rosie did a great job of coping with Aunt Maud's nosiness and calmly praised his parenting skills. Rosie agreed how proud they should all be of Lisa and declared with a tight smile that Nashville was her home now.

Did she agree to have dinner with him tonight simply as a sop to his ego? Jack pushed his way through to the kitchen and made his escape via the back door.

'You would not think it was February.' Gino sprawled on one of the patio chairs, stretching out his long legs and tilting back his head to catch a few rays of watery sunshine. 'It is not unlike winter in Sicily where my grandparents have a home.'

'You're lucky — it could've been freezing cold and tipping it down.'

'I know I am lucky, Jack, in far more ways than the weather.'

'Don't tell me you've abandoned Lisa already?'

Gino levered back up to standing and ran a hand over his enviably obedient hair.

'She's gone upstairs with one of her bridesmaids.' He grinned. 'Apparently princess dresses do not easily squash into bathrooms without help so I was ordered to get some fresh air for ten minutes.' He tapped his watch.

'Two minutes and thirty seconds left.' A shadow filtered across Gino's smile. 'I will be a good husband to Lisa. You have my promise.'

Jack's throat tightened.

Gino gestured towards the house.

'Are you coming back in? I believe it is almost time for the cake and speeches.'

'Of course.' The well-mannered young man must be curious why Jack had come outside in the first place. 'A touch of fresh air sounded tempting to me, too.'

'Ms Rosie is quite a woman.'

Alarm bells sounded in Jack's head. Had his daughter ordered her new husband to probe if he got the chance to discover Jack's feelings?

'I am not asking for Lisa.' Gino's perception knocked Jack sideways. 'Some things are meant and we cannot argue with it.' Gino shrugged. 'Your daughter set her sights on me and went like a heavy rolling thing over my heart.'

'You mean a steamroller.' Jack laughed. 'She resembles her mother that way. Rosie always went for what she wanted until she got it . . . He slapped his son-in-law's back. 'Forget all that — you've got no worries with Lisa. She learned from my mistakes.'

'Are you sure is it too late for you and Rosie?'

'Probably.'

Gino nudged him.

'Maybe tonight you use the romance of the day to plant the seed and then you come to Rome at the same time Lisa's mother visits? Italy casts a magic spell on many lovers. I am proof of that.'

'For a man who's only been married for a couple of hours you're very sure of yourself.' The other man's face split into a wide smile.

'Let us go. If I do not get my hands on that delicious cannoli cake soon I will not be responsible for my behaviour.'

★   ★   ★

Despite Rosie's best efforts, Jack's voice drifted into the kitchen because everyone else fell silent, caught up in his eloquent heartfelt speech with poignant memories from Lisa's childhood entwined with pride in the woman she'd grown into.

The breath caught in her throat when Rosie picked out her name, leading her to draw closer to the open kitchen door.

'Rosie and I love Lisa with all our hearts. We always have and always will and now encompass Gino in the same enduring love. On behalf of us both I ask you to raise your glasses and toast the happy couple. To Lisa and Gino.'

'Here you go.' Liam, Bruno's second in command, pressed a glass of champagne into her hand.

Through a film of tears she nodded her thanks and took a sip of the sparkling wine. Propelled by something outside herself. Rosie stepped into the main room and ignored the sideways glances to make her way to the front.

'If no-one minds I'd like to say a few words.' Catching a glimpse of her mother's anxious face Rosie managed a tiny smile.

'Everyone here knows I haven't been the mother Lisa deserved but she still had Jack, the best father any girl could ever have. This is a toast to him because without the unstinting love he devoted to raising his daughter ... ' Rosie's voice threatened to give way and she cleared her throat, determined to get through this without breaking down.

'She wouldn't be the amazing woman she is today.' Rosie raised her glass and steeled her arm to remain steady. 'To Jack.'

After everyone joined in Rosie froze, desperate to disappear back to the kitchen but almost suffocated by the people crowding around, suddenly keen to talk to her. A warm hand grasped her arm and she tilted her head to meet Jack's electric blue eyes.

'You'll all have to take a turn chatting to Rosie later. For now she's ours.' Leaving everyone, including Rosie, with no choice, he steered her away.

'You were spot on there, Mum.' Lisa let go of her new husband and threw her arms around Rosie.

'You'll crush your dress.'

'I don't care.'

'I don't deserve . . . '

'Yes, you do.' Lisa's insistence brought more tears bubbling to the surface and they trickled down, bringing a river of mascara with them. 'Your toast was brave and you're absolutely right about Dad.'

Rosie eased out of her daughter's embrace and smoothed down the front of her wedding gown.

'Don't forget the cake cutting. Your husband will rip it apart with his bare hands if you don't hurry up.'

Her forced laughter came with an unspoken plea to leave any deep conversation for another day. Lisa's grey eyes darkened to the same smoky shade as her own.

'My mother-in-law is right,' Gino piped up in a subtle effort to break the impasse.

'Hey, you should record that, Rosie. It might not be a phrase you hear very often.' Jack slipped his arm around her shoulder and his heat and familiar clean scent seeped into her awareness.

With the same engraved silver Kitto family knife Rosie and Jack had used at their own wedding, the improvised cake was cut and taken away ready to be passed around to the guests.

'I should go and help.' Rosie suggested.

'You're not going anywhere. You've more than done your part and Bruno's people are totally capable.'

'You've become bossy in middle age.'

'And you're as stubborn as ever.' His charming smile swept away any hint of real annoyance. 'Another hour and this will all be over then it's our time.'

'Don't be daft. Everything's got to be cleared up and your house restored to normal.' Rosie glanced away and then shook her head. 'Oh, heavens, our mothers are watching us and looking unbearably smug.'

Walking in the Sand

'Wow, is the sophisticated Rosalind look put on for my benefit?' Jack struggled to sound casual and somehow suppressed the urge to jump to his feet. Instead he took his time folding the newspaper and laying it on the coffee table before standing.

'As you're the man I'm going out with tonight I'll go for a yes.'

The sleek mulberry silk clung to every subtle curve with a discreet side slit hinting at long toned legs. Posed on the last stair she could feature on a magazine cover.

'I surrender.' Playfully he threw his arms up in the air. 'You win.'

'Oh, you're no fun.' Rosie mock-pouted. 'The battle is half the challenge.' She glanced around. 'House back to normal?'

'The furniture is. My life not so much.'

'Oh.'

'Shall we go?' Jack's heartbeat thudded against his chest while he waited for Rosie to take his outstretched hand. 'You mentioned the Gull House in Falmouth the other day so I've booked us a table there.'

'Wow, how did you manage that?'

'Hey, you're not the only one with connections.' Making Rosie see him in a different light was crucial in his plot to win her back. 'By the way, what's your mother doing tonight?'

'She's hanging out with yours and no doubt they're hatching a pile of trouble.'

If Jack dared to smile he knew she'd smack him but later he'd be sure to give Eliza and Maggie an extra hug.

Initially distrustful of Rosie's return, his mother was now firmly of the belief that their divorce and 25-year separation were little more than a blip in the path of true love.

'Maybe with Valentine's Day coming up next week they've got romance on their minds.'

'Fools,' Rosie scoffed. 'You'd think they'd know better at their age.'

'I don't get it. How come you're in the wedding business when you're such a cynic? Or is that a cover up for . . . '

'Are you taking me to dinner or should I go take off this dress and fix myself a peanut-butter sandwich?'

'Sorry.' Jack grinned. 'Anyway my kitchen is a peanut-butter-free zone so you'd be out of luck.'

She trailed her gaze down over him and the same long remembered wicked glint sparkled in her eyes.

'Oh, I'm pretty sure I'm in luck.' Suddenly a touch of uncertainly seeped into her smile. 'Are we mad?'

'Don't get ahead of us. No pressure. No expectations.'

'Hope?'

Jack couldn't lie.

'Of course. Don't you? Would you have accepted my invitation otherwise?'

'Maybe not.' A flood of colour heated her face to scorching level. 'I'd have made up a story about being too tired or already seeing someone but . . . '

'You couldn't lie.'

Rosie shook her head and his heart sung the 'Hallelujah Chorus' at full volume.

'That's good. Let's go.' Jack left it there. Sometimes less was more.

★ ★ ★

'Wow, that was insanely good.' Scraping out the last bite of crème brûlée, Rosie licked the spoon. 'This place is even better than the reviews promised.'

She gazed around the elegant restaurant and through the floor-to-ceiling windows at the stunning view of Falmouth harbour, the deepest natural harbour in Europe.

A myriad of sailboats bobbed in the black star-spangled water bracketed by the Maritime Museum and ancient town.

'I'd be the size of a house if I stayed in Cornwall long.' The sight of Jack's taut jawline brought her another sliver of regret. Every word they spoke resembled tentative steps across a minefield and at this rate they wouldn't reach the other side unscathed.

'Coffee?'

'Do you know what I'd really love?' Rosie reached for his hand.

'To walk on Gyllyngvase beach again and dip your toes in the freezing water?'

She couldn't hide her surprise at his accurate mind-reading.

'You were always a cheap date. Give you damp sand and an ice-cream and you're a happy girl.'

'You could have saved a bundle by skipping dinner and going straight for the good stuff.'

'Too late now.' Jack laughed and quickly caught the waiter's eye to ask for the bill. 'We're not exactly dressed for paddling.'

'Don't tell me you're too middle-aged to live dangerously?'

'Would I be here now if I was?' His darkening eyes narrowed and a tingle of excitement shivered through her.

'It's only a five-minute drive. Let's go.'

Before she could question him again about the wisdom of all this Rosie found herself back in Jack's car and being driven through the empty streets.

Nine o'clock in the evening on a chilly mid-February night must rank as one of the lowest points of the tourist season. That meant plenty of open parking spaces next to the slipway giving access to the broad crescent of golden sand, rated as one of Cornwall's best beaches.

'I'm leaving my shoes here.' Jack propped his door open and stuck his long legs outside.

Rosie made quick work of slipping out of her own high heels. She buttoned up her short black wool jacket against the blustery wind gusting in from the sea.

'Remember the last time we came here?'

She squeezed Jack's outstretched hand.

'Don't. Please.' After two months they'd barely settled into married life when a visit to her doctor revealed the shocking diagnosis that her upset stomach was in fact an unplanned honeymoon baby.

Rosie vividly remembered fretting all week over how to break the news to Jack but he guessed the minute she'd opened up their picnic lunch on the beach and turned nauseous at the smell of their egg sandwiches. Twenty-five years later Jack's ecstatic reaction still stuck in her mind.

'Isn't it better than keeping it buried inside the rest of our lives?' He wrapped her in his warm arms and her head nestled in the familiar curve of his shoulder.

'If we'd been more honest at the time, things might've been different. I behaved like a typical puffed-up teen-age boy, proud of what I saw as proof of being a man.'

Jack smoothed a hand over her hair.

'It didn't click with me that the idea

of becoming a mother before you were ready scared you. You saw it ending our dreams of escaping from Cornwall as soon as we got some money together.' He cracked a wry smile. 'You were spot on. I never did.'

'Did you want to?'

'Want to? Maybe . . . '

'But you needed help taking care of Lisa. Don't sugar-coat it, Jack. I'm the very last person with the right to criticise or question your choices.' Rosie sucked in a breath and slowly exhaled. 'And what about now?'

'Let's walk.'

'I thought we . . . '

'We are talking, Rosie. Don't push too fast.' He tweaked her nose. 'Cold, damp sand — come on, how can you resist?' Jack looped her arm through his and gave an encouraging smile. 'One step at a time.'

She conceded with a brief nod and they made their way down on to the beach to find themselves unsurprisingly the only people strolling under the moonlit sky. By silent mutual agreement they stopped halfway along to stare out to the horizon and Rosie snuggled back into Jack's embrace.

'What's Nashville like?'

'You could come and see.'

'I'd like that.'

'Let's be realistic.' Not for the first time she resented being so practical but the reckless side of her nature shrivelled up years ago after too much misuse. 'You can't abandon your mother and I'm not going to ditch my career.'

'Oh, Rosie.' Jack turned to face her, stroking his thumb down her cheek to linger on the pulse in her neck. 'Life isn't cut and dried. Believe it or not, there are aeroplanes that cross the Atlantic these days in a matter of hours.'

'Very funny.'

'You've talked about expanding your business to Europe. I'm my own boss. Are you closing the door on even exploring the possibility of . . . '

'Breaking our hearts again?' She

strode off down the beach and didn't wait to see if he followed. The tide lapped at her toes and she plunged in up past her ankles. 'Good grief, I'd forgotten how cold the water is here.'

Jack made a grab for her arm and swung her back around to face his burning eyes.

'Didn't stop you running in, though, did it? You can be brave about us, too.'

'Why are you so certain?'

The question stuck deep in Jack's core and he suspected this might be the most important answer he ever gave. He slid his hand in between her coat buttons to rest against her thudding heart.

'Because of this. Can you honestly say you've loved any other man since me?' In the faint moonlight, her cheeks turned pink.

'I've dated.'

'That's not what I asked.' He'd share his story first and see if that helped. 'I've never told another woman I loved her because I couldn't lie. There was one I thought I might be able to care for . . . but in the end it didn't work out.'

'How can you ever get past what I did to you and Lisa?'

Other people saw a confident successful woman but under the skin Rosie remained the petrified seventeen-year-old girl who ran away for a multitude of heartbreaking reasons.

'You really think we're the first young couple to make mistakes?' Jack needed her to understand he wasn't perfect and never had been. 'Pay attention to the fact I said 'we'. You've dumped all the blame on yourself far too long.'

A protest hovered on her lips but he ploughed on.

'We both needed to grow up. If you hadn't left, who says we could've made our marriage work for the long haul? We might've been lucky but there aren't any guarantees.' He risked a soft kiss on her lips. 'Life doesn't come with them, sweetheart.'

'What do you think Lisa will say if we

. . . I mean . . . '

Hearing her stumble kicked his hopes back into high gear.

'You need to hear what she said to me earlier today when we were alone for a few minutes. Lisa admitted she'd been wary meeting you again because growing up she protected herself by swearing that she didn't need a mother in her life.

'You've turned her preconceptions upside down and Gino helped her to see that forming a relationship with you now isn't a betrayal of me or her totally valid feelings of sadness for what could've been.'

He touched her chin, tilting it so she couldn't avoid looking at him.

'Lisa told me we look right together.' Jack didn't need a mirror to know his face resembled a red traffic light. He shuffled his feet, now he found it hard to face Rosie head on. 'Her exact words were 'For heaven's sake, Daddy, don't use me or anything else as an excuse. Go for it.''

'Oh.'

A touch of wariness crept into her eyes.

'What are you asking?'

'Good question. For a start — don't go out with the famous chef tomorrow.'

'But after all he did to help out with the reception I can't . . . '

'Yes, you can. I'm sorry but if he needs thanking I'll send him a bottle of whisky along with the large cheque I owe him.'

'I've never heard you sound all macho before.'

He folded his arms.

'Would you be happy if I went out with another woman?'

'No,' Rosie conceded, 'but I wouldn't consider it my right to stop you.'

The last time Jack felt this nervous was when he had got down on one knee while brandishing the tiniest diamond ring in the history of the planet, hoping the woman now staring at him would agree to his crazy proposal.

Old Enough to Know Better

This wasn't part of the plan to fly into London for her father's funeral, stay long enough to make sure her mum was OK then return to Nashville and her regular life.

'You're going to Plymouth for your work so why not run on down to St Wenn?' her mother had said.

If Rosie had used her common sense and turned down her mother's suggestion this unbreakable connection with Jack would have stayed tucked away in an untouched corner of her heart.

But no, she'd been persuaded to revisit the past and their long suppressed love had burst into bloom again, only growing stronger by the hour.

She succumbed to a heavy sigh.

'I'll call Bruno, OK?' The satisfied smile spreading across his face deserved a smack but instead she planted a decisive kiss on his tempting mouth to make her feelings absolutely clear.

'You realise I've got to return to Nashville in the next few days or my business partner will beat a path to Cornwall and drag me on a plane?'

'I need to get back to work too.' His upper lip curled. 'I hear Rome is particularly lovely in April.'

'A lot of research will be needed if Wedding Wishes is to branch out.' Rosie couldn't hold back a wide grin. 'There are a lot of Italian-Americans who'd love to get married in the old country but don't know how to go about it.'

'I'm sure you could teach them a thing or two.' Jack's snappy response made her blush. 'I don't know about you but I can't feel my feet any more. I'm pretty sure they've turned into blocks of ice.

'Does the idea of going back to my warm house hold any appeal? I could whip us up some of my exceptional hot chocolate.'

Rosie's eyes stung and she blinked away a cloud of tears. She remembered Jack's hot chocolate was practically a work of art that involved melting good dark chocolate over a double boiler before whisking it into milk steeped with sugar, vanilla and a cinnamon stick.

On the few occasions they could afford for Jack to make it, his final flourish was a swirl of whipped cream and a further sprinkling of chocolate. Because of its connection with her handsome young husband she'd never touched it since.

'It appeals very much.'

'Good.' A flare of longing exploded in his eyes. 'You know you appeal to me too, right?'

'Oh yeah. Ditto.' Rosie broke into a nervous laugh. 'I'm not much for romance — as you can tell.'

'I'll teach you.' Sweeping her into his arms, Jack ignored her shrieks and ran as fast as he could back to the car. After he set her down he fought to catch his breath. 'I must get back to exercising regularly. I bet you're in the gym every day and probably run marathons too.'

Her teenage self preferred cuddling with Jack on the sofa while sharing a bag of chips to anything overly energetic. A lot had changed.

'You'll be a good influence on me.'

'It works both ways. These days I'm not good at relaxing which isn't healthy.' Rosie shivered. 'Open the car for heaven's sake or you'll be taking home an ice maiden.'

He leaned in for another red-hot kiss.

'Nope, definitely not an ice maiden.' Jack dangled the keys in the air. 'Let's get our shoes back on I'll put the heater on full blast followed very soon by hot chocolate.'

★   ★   ★

'I thought you were going to a fancy restaurant — not paddling on the beach?'

Before Rosie could refute her mother's accusation, she glanced at her bare, sand-crusted legs and realised they'd been rumbled.

'The pair of them never did have an atom of common sense,' Eliza joined in.

They'd discovered both women drinking tea in the kitchen when they crept into the house and the conversation had come to an abrupt halt, replaced by quiet, knowing smiles.

'Well?' Maggie persisted. 'Have you got any news for us?'

Rosie could drag it out and make her mother work for the information but that verged on cruel. Rosie took Jack's shoulder shrug as permission to say as much or as little as she wanted.

'We've really talked this evening and cleared up a lot of misunderstanding but — and it's a big but — we're not rushing into anything.' She wasn't sure why Jack's smile faltered and disappointment emanated from him in waves.

'We've already done that and caused

ourselves and a lot of other people, including both of you, a bunch of heartache. We're thinking of going to Rome together in April to visit Lisa and Gino. After that, we'll see.'

'I know that makes sense but you aren't getting any younger.' Jack's outspoken mother didn't mince her words. 'For goodness sake, don't waste too long faffing about.'

'Eliza's right.'

'Thanks, Mum.' Rosie's touch of sarcasm did the trick and her mother fell quiet. 'If you fancy hot chocolate Jack's making some.'

'Hear that, Maggie?' Eliza scoffed. 'In other words, we've been told to mind our own business because they're old enough to work it out themselves.' She pushed her chair away and scrabbled around by her feet for the ancient tapestry bag she'd hauled around ever since Rosie could remember.

'We'll see you tomorrow at one o'clock for lunch at the Red Lion.'

Rosie barely managed to suppress a

giggle as Jack mimed a dramatic bow behind his mother's back.

'I'm looking forward to it,' Rosie said.

'Would you like a ride home, Mum?' Jack asked.

Eliza rolled her eyes at her son.

'Good grief, I'm not past it yet. It's a five-minute walk.'

'I'm off to bed,' Maggie announced and went over to rinse her tea mug in the sink.

'We'll see you both tomorrow.' Jack slipped his arm around Rosie's waist and something in his firm tone registered because in a flurry of hugs and goodbyes they were left alone again. 'Before you say anything I'm sorry I acted like a spoiled kid when you answered your mum's question. That was juvenile.'

'Yep, it was.' Not that such fast agreement would help his ego. 'But sort of cute.'

'Cute, eh?'

'Wipe the smirk off your face.' Rosie

ordered but the warning arrived with a faint hint of amusement. 'I meant every word. Are you ever going to make the hot chocolate you promised? At this rate we'll be drinking it for breakfast.'

Watching the sunrise with Rosie didn't strike Jack as a bad way to start a day but he wasn't daft enough to say so.

'Make yourself comfortable and watch a genius at work.'

'Oh, really? Where do I find one of those?'

He'd missed this. Nothing matched the comfortable back and forth between two people who knew each other inside out. He wasn't stupid. They'd a long way to go and weren't the crazy in-love teenagers of a quarter century ago but that wasn't important.

Rosie had closed her eyes for a moment. It had been a long day.

'Open your eyes, love, open your eyes.' With an exaggerated flip of her long lashes Rosie's smoky gaze rested on him.

'Like that?'

The low hum of her raspy voice slid over his skin and it took all his self-control to reach down a block of chocolate from the cupboard and pull out the grater.

'You are trouble.'

'Only now worked that one out?'

'No, I cottoned on to it the day you suddenly professed an interest in drama and showed up at all my rehearsals in your skimpy mesh dress, patterned tights and Doc Marten boots. Although I'm relieved you abandoned the over-permed hair, butterfly clips and frosted lipstick in your efforts to lure me in.'

'Do you forget nothing?' Rosie pressed her hands against her hot cheeks. 'What about the awful blond highlights you put in your hair along with a truckload of gel? I'm guessing it was supposed to make you look like God's gift to women?'

'Worked, though, didn't it, because I got you?' The words slipped out before he could think of pulling them back.

'Don't apologise. We've gotta get past

the urge to do that over and over if we're going to make a go of this.'

'You're right.' Jack returned to his cooking magic, sensing her attention focused on him but refusing to keep turning around to check. 'There you go.' He set two mugs down on the table and pulled out a chair to sit by her. 'This is Lisa's favourite, too.'

'Is it?'

The touch of wistfulness undid him.

'It's OK.' She covered his hand with her own, curling her long fingers around and tucking them in tight. 'When we've more time you can fill me in. I'll never know it all and I can live with that . . . ' Rosie gave him a questioning glance ' . . . as long as you can too?'

'We'll make new memories.' Jack grinned. 'Starting now.' He scooped a blob of whipped cream on his finger and plopped it on the end of her nose. 'Got you.'

'Oh, it's like that is it, Jack Kitto?' Before he could duck she followed suit and deposited a large splat of cream on his forehead followed by a broad swipe down his face.

'You'll wish you hadn't done that.' He grabbed the aerosol can off the counter and sprayed an arc of whipped cream over her hair.

'Whatever's all the noise about?' Maggie frowned at them from the doorway. 'For goodness' sake, act your ages.'

'Why?' They chimed back and squeezed together in a sticky hug.

'Your dear mother hit the nail on the head, Jack,' Maggie said. 'Nobody else would take the pair of you on. You've proved that all these years. I'll see you both in the morning.' With a smug smile she left them to it.

'Think they're right?' Jack ventured.

'They usually are.' The thought didn't appear to excite Rosie until a girlish giggle escaped. 'Does it freak you out too?'

'Not any longer.' He kissed away a smudge of cream from her lips.

'Me neither. It's been quite a day.'

Jack glanced at their abandoned drinks.

'That's the last time I make you hot chocolate.'

'Spoilsport. Don't tell me you're not going to be any fun in your old age?'

'I hope you'll stick around to find out.'

'I hope so too.'

The older, wiser Jack didn't push.

'Italy casts a magic spell on many lovers,' Gino had said. Fingers crossed that Rome in the springtime would seal the deal.

Time to Celebrate

'Not quite Elm Terrace, is it?' Rosie's bemused smile forced Jack to choke down a fit of laughter.

The newlyweds' luxurious fifth floor apartment in the Campo de' Fiori was far more than the geographical 1,400 miles from the tiny rundown cottage where they started their own married life.

Marble floors instead of threadbare carpet and an eclectic mix of elegant antiques and sleek modern styling as opposed to the motley collection of second-hand furniture scrounged from their families.

'I hope you don't mind too dreadfully but I need to go into work.' Lisa rushed in, still in the middle of tugging on her high-heeled black shoes.

'I planned to take the day off but there's a big presentation tomorrow and

I need to be sure I'm on top of things. We thought you'd be happy to stay in tonight for dinner and eat earlier than usual for Mum's sake.'

'We'll be fine. Off you go.'

'Thanks, Daddy.' The slight blink of hesitation almost went unnoticed but he knew her too well. 'I'm really glad you've come, Mum.'

'So am I.'

A thread of tension hummed around the two women he loved and Jack couldn't help wondering how long it would take for them to be at ease with each other.

After the front door slammed behind Lisa — some things never changed — he hardly dared look at Rosie.

Two months wasn't a long time according to the calendar but each day gave him more scope for missing her and worrying. The hundreds of phone calls, texts and emails they exchanged couldn't allay the niggling fear that she'd change her mind about them.

He'd told himself over and over that

the nervous knot in his stomach would disappear when he held her in his arms again and looked into her eyes. Then he'd know for sure.

'If you . . . '

'I'm not . . . '

Trying to both talk at the same time broke through the awkwardness and Jack regained the nerve he'd lost when she walked out of the arrivals gate at the airport, blending in with the elegant Italian women in her dark skinny jeans and white blouse topped with a loose pale pink knitted jacket.

Tan ankle boots and splash of scarlet lipstick completed the non-American tourist look.

'Have you gone off me?' Rosie's quizzical tilt of the head took him aback.

'Gone off you?' Jack croaked. 'Are you mad?'

'I've been here . . . ' She made a point of checking her watch. 'Two hours. That's a hundred and twenty endless minutes and you haven't kissed me yet.'

'I'll happily . . . ' Before he could finish Jack discovered that the scarlet lips tasted of strawberries and despite spending the last 12 plus hours travelling, Rosie's fresh citrusy scent lingered to stir his senses.

Surfacing from the kiss he'd dreamed about for far too many long nights he gave an exaggerated sigh.

'Wow. Better than I remember.'

'Yeah well, at your advanced age I suppose I'll take what I can get.' Rosie settled in his arms.

'As I tried to say, I'm not tired so you can take me out for lunch and show me some of the sights.'

'I don't know how you do it. It's less than a three-hour flight from London to Rome and still Lisa had to pack me off to bed at eight o'clock last night when I practically fell asleep in the pasta.'

'No caffeine for twenty-four hours before flying. Wear comfortable clothes. Request a window seat. Tell the attendant you don't want to be disturbed unless it's an emergency.' A satisfied grin crept over her face. 'Invest in good eyeshades and noise-cancelling headphones.'

'Sounds like a battle plan.'

'Flying transatlantic these days needs one. Don't forget that when . . . I mean if . . . ' Rosie's colour deepened.

Jack cupped her face, spreading his fingers through her shiny dark hair.

'WHEN I come, I promise to follow your golden rules.'

Rosie's cold feet and all the jittery bits between calmed down. They'd spent so many years apart yet still read each other better than anyone else.

As soon as their mutual sense of humour clicked again, the shadows darkening his eyes to an impenetrable navy blue cleared.

It didn't need spelling out that they had both spent the last couple of months over-thinking what they were or weren't up to.

'My business partner, Crispin, can't wait to meet you. He reckons you waved a magic wand and turned me back into a normal human being.'

Jack's broad smile encouraged her to share the rest of her news.

'We're going ahead with our expansion plans for Wedding Wishes and I'm going to head up our European arm.'

'Great. You didn't waste any time. My business isn't quite as flexible.' Heat blossomed on his face. 'That doesn't mean I wouldn't abandon it all . . . for us.' Jack grabbed her hands, pulling them against his chest. 'I'm not messing things up with you a second time.'

'But you weren't the one . . . '

'Hey, you've got to agree once and for all that in our case it took two and then leave it alone.'

Did Jack understand what a huge thing he asked of her? Rosie met his searching gaze and couldn't help smiling. Of course he knew.

If they couldn't climb that particular obstacle together, nothing else mattered but as long as they succeeded then nothing could stop them.

'Rosie?'

'I may still have wobbles on some days. Can you . . . of course you'll be patient with me.' Tears pricked her eyes. 'You've always been a patient man, Jack. More so than I . . . Rosie slapped her hand over her mouth and muttered through her closed fingers.

'Sorry. Not supposed to say things like that any more.'

'Good girl.' The last tiny lingering doubt disappeared into his lingering kiss. 'I'll take you to Luigi's for lunch. I ate there with Lisa and Gino last night and it's amazing.

'It's only a five-minute walk and we can easily go on from there to the Spanish Steps, the Trevi Fountain or the Vatican. Pretty much anywhere you fancy in the centre of the city.

'See how you feel but remember we've got until Friday and don't have to cram everything in today.' Jack's voice softened. 'I understand your desire to see as much as we can. Life is a bit like an egg timer with the sand running out.'

'Boy, aren't you Mr Cheerful?'

'Hey,' he shrugged, 'we've wasted enough grains already and I'm with you on not squandering any more.' Another breathtaking kiss caught her out, in the best possible way. 'That covers a multitude of subjects, including pizza.'

Rosie stomach rumbled.

'You mentioned the tantalising word so it's totally your fault.'

'Guilty as charged. I'll lead you to a plate of the best pizza you've ever tasted. They cook it in a centuries-old brick oven and it only takes a couple of minutes.'

Oh, Jack I'd follow you anywhere pizza or no pizza. Her cheeks burned as she saw him read her thoughts.

'Lead away.'

★ ★ ★

Jack shifted his leg to get the blood flowing again without disturbing Rosie, sprawled out fast asleep with her head cradled in his lap on the sofa. They'd walked off their lunch and more until she finally admitted defeat.

'It's been wonderful finally getting to see all these places I've heard about and longed to visit,' Rosie had said on their way back to the apartment.

'For years I didn't have the money to travel and now I've the money but refused to make the time. You're good for me, Jack.'

The three small words he longed to say came to the tip of his tongue but he bit them back, saving them for the right moment.

'Hey, Daddy . . . '

'Shush.' Jack pointed down at Rosie and his daughter made a similar gesture to Gino over her shoulder. Keeping his voice to a whisper he explained all they'd done and dropped a hint that a cup of tea might not go amiss.

'I'll make us one. I haven't converted my dear husband yet to the joys of tea

244

drinking.' A few minutes in the kitchen and Lisa returned with two mugs, then curled up on the floor by his feet.

'You've changed,' she told her father.

'For good or bad?'

'Definitely good,' Lisa insisted. 'Maybe it's because I'm out of your hair and you can be more you again.' She stopped his attempt to protest. 'I actually think it's more to do with Mum. You really want to be with her again, don't you?' The blunt statement floored him. 'It's OK. I don't mind.' A tiny frown creased her forehead. 'I did at first but Gino's helped me through that.'

'Are you sure?'

'Absolutely. I love you and I . . . I'm growing to love her, too.' A tinge of colour heightened Lisa's sharp cheekbones, the mirror image of her mother's. 'I think you'll both make amazing grandparents.'

Rosie jerked up and Jack's mug soared in the air splattering hot tea everywhere.

'Grandparents? You're going to have a baby?'

Lisa beamed and took hold of Gino's outstretched hand to let him pull her to her feet.

'That's usually what it means and before you ask we absolutely wanted to start a family right away.'

'I wouldn't dream of . . . '

'How long were you awake before the um . . . baby revelation?' Jack's tentative question turned Rosie's cheeks the same shade as her name.

'Long enough but we'll talk later. First I want to hear all about this baby.'

So much for his plan to build up to his big declaration over the next few days.

Gino gently stroked Lisa's flat stomach.

'Our little one will arrive in November.'

As the baby chatter continued, Jack brushed away a stray tear. If he'd received this news before he'd be wondering whether to let Rosie know

246

the big news and now miraculously they were celebrating together. Jack glanced up to catch the clear emotion burning in Rosie's luminous eyes.

'I am making my lovely wife take a rest,' Gino wagged a finger, 'she is not good at that. After we will have dinner.'

'I'll clear up the mugs and everything.' Rosie frowned at the stains darkening the pristine white sofa.

'I'm afraid it might need professional cleaning. I'm so sorry.'

'Do not worry. Take a bottle of Prosecco out on the balcony and enjoy the view.' He winked at Jack. 'I'm sure you have a lot to talk about.'

Second Time Around

'Stand still, Mum.' Lisa remonstrated with Rosie while tucking a stray curl back in place. 'At least you haven't had a wardrobe malfunction yet.'

No way would she get through today without crying but Rosie's fervent hope that it'd be later than 11 o'clock in the morning failed at the sight of her beautiful daughter.

The baby bump pressing against the creamy yellow floral silk shift dress brought all her emotions flooding to the surface.

'Stop the tears right now — we don't have time to re-do your make-up.' Lisa smoothed a hand over Rosie's hair. 'Daddy will be such a wreck when he sees you.'

Poor Jack had lived in a constant state of wreckedness — if that was even a word — since April when he'd been catapulted into proclaiming his love on her first night in Rome.

'He's looking pretty handsome himself today.' Lisa grinned.

'The custom-made Italian suit helps although I suspect you wouldn't care if he turned up in the old jeans he wears to do the garden.'

Rosie couldn't deny it because she'd fancied Jack since she was sixteen. No man ever touched her soul the same way and anything less wasn't worth having.

'The dress works, doesn't it?'

Not a fan of second-time brides who chose traditional white dresses or dreary pastel outfits more suited to an old-fashioned mother of the bride she'd haunted Pinterest until her laptop almost blew up.

Finally a short, simple and stunning vintage dress caught her eye that ticked every box. A sleeveless ivory lace bodice covered the tea-length tulle flared dress in the unusual colour of a rich latte and cinched at the waist with a matching satin belt.

'You know it does but I'll play the reassuring matron of honour anyway.'

'Thanks.' Rosie's heart overflowed with so many things she ached to say but Lisa shook her head.

'We're going to see each other lots from now on. Let's be patient.'

'How did you get to be so wise? Don't tell me — learning from your parents' mistakes.'

Before Lisa could answer, a sharp rap on the bedroom door interrupted the conversation.

'The car's here!' Rosie's mother yelled in from the hall. 'Do I get to see the bride?'

'Of course. Come in.' Rosie wasn't at ease with everyone making such a fuss of her but determined not to spoil Maggie's pleasure.

'Eliza's here too.'

Since reconnecting at Lisa's wedding they'd become close friends again and it lifted Rosie's spirits to see Maggie adjusting to widowhood better thanks to Jack's exuberant mother.

'Oh my, I love the dress.'

'It's not the dress, dearie.' Eliza's smile broadened. 'Not that I don't like it — because I do.' She touched her hand to Rosie's cheek. 'It's love making her beautiful. I only regret you had to go through . . . '

'No regrets today.' The conviction in Rosie's voice silenced everyone. 'Today Jack and I are drawing a line under the past and starting a new life together.

'What's done can't be undone. We've changed and grown because of it and we're ready to recommit to each other.'

'Bravo, Mum.' Lisa clapped her hands. 'Now let's get going and rescue my poor father before he gnaws every fingernail down to the quick.'

* * *

When Rosie had suggested getting married in the village church Jack had been wary and suggested they chose a different venue, perhaps even go to Rome.

'That strikes me as running away and I'm never doing that again,' Rosie had said. 'I want to stand up in front of everyone we care for and proclaim my love for you and hear you do the same in return.'

The organist played the first notes of Handel's 'Water Music', Rosie's choice because she claimed she'd hated 'Here Comes The Bride' since it had been played on a tinny CD player in the registry office their first time around.

Standing at the end of aisle with a radiant smile aimed straight at him, the sight of his love made Jack's heart race.

No longer the gawky, uncertain teenager who won his sixteen-year-old heart but now a beautiful confident woman who knew what she wanted and — crazily enough — it was still him.

When Rosie reached his side, Lisa took her mother's bouquet of cream rosebuds and flashed them both a quick approving smile.

The soft touch of Rosie's hand and hint of her familiar perfume helped to steady his nerves and before long they recited their wedding vows, exchanging a tiny smile as they reached the part about 'so long as you both shall live'.

'You may kiss the bride.'

Jack didn't need telling twice and cupped his hands around her face, drawing her to him for a long, lingering kiss before reluctantly letting go.

'Ready, Mrs Kitto?'

'Oh, yes.'

Half an hour later he decided he'd been photographed from every possible angle. No cheap Instamatic snapshots today.

'I wish we had a longer drive to the reception.'

After the success of Lisa's hastily arranged party, they'd decided to hold their own reception back at Tregony House.

Bruno happily offered to take charge after first having a good laugh about not standing in the way of true love.

'You'll have plenty of time on the flight to Nashville for talking.'

'Talking? I suppose we can do that too.' Jack grinned. A sharp jab in the ribs told him to behave.

They would spend their wedding night in London and fly out tomorrow to spend a fortnight introducing Jack to his new bride's other home.

From now on, she'd spend the majority of her time in Cornwall while working all around Europe to find unique venues for Wedding Wishes.

Crispin and a new partner would concentrate on the original business.

'Did I tell you how beautiful you are today?' Jack helped her into the white Rolls-Royce, one of the impossibly expensive dreams she had at sixteen that he'd finally fulfilled today.

'Yes, but please feel free to say so again. We soon-to-be grandmothers need all the reassurance we can get that we're not past it.'

Jack chuckled.

'Trust me — no-one will believe that

of you. Anyway, what about me? I was considering buying slippers and dying my hair grey to look the part.'

'Of a grandmother? You'll need a heck of a lot more than that to do the trick.'

'Very funny, I'm sure.'

Rosie snuggled into him in the back seat.

'If you're searching for compliments . . . in my eyes you'll be the hottest grandfather ever and this particular grandmother won't be able to keep her hands off you.'

'That's the plan, Mrs Kitto.'

Since the day Rosie had walked into the Old Goose pub and back into Jack's life he'd dreamed of them becoming a family again, no longer separated by time and misunderstanding.

It was a dream he had never for a moment imagined would be fulfilled, but it just went to show that you never knew what life had in store for you.

Sometimes it wasn't necessary to win the lottery to hit the jackpot.

We do hope that you have enjoyed reading this large print book.

Did you know that all of our titles are available for purchase?

We publish a wide range of high quality large print books including:
Romances, Mysteries, Classics
General Fiction
Non Fiction and Westerns

Special interest titles available in large print are:
The Little Oxford Dictionary
Music Book, Song Book
Hymn Book, Service Book

Also available from us courtesy of Oxford University Press:
Young Readers' Dictionary
(large print edition)
Young Readers' Thesaurus
(large print edition)

For further information or a free brochure, please contact us at:
Ulverscroft Large Print Books Ltd.,
The Green, Bradgate Road, Anstey,
Leicester, LE7 7FU, England.
Tel: (00 44) **0116 236 4325**
Fax: (00 44) **0116 234 0205**

A LITTLE BIT OF
CHRISTMAS MAGIC

Kirsty Ferry

As a wedding planner at Carrick Park Hotel, Ailsa McCormack is organising a Christmas Day wedding at the expense of her own holiday. Not that she minds. She's always been fascinated by the place and its past occupants; particularly the beautiful and tragic Ella Carrick, whose striking portrait still hangs at the top of the stairs. And then an encounter with a tall, handsome and strangely familiar man in the drawing room on Christmas Eve sets off a chain of events that transforms Ailsa's lonely Christmas into a magical occasion . . .

DOCTOR'S LEGACY

Phyllis Mallett

When Dr Helen Farley arrives in the Cornish fishing village of Tredporth as a locum, she feels instantly at home, and is fascinated by the large house standing on the cliffs. Owned by the ageing Edsel Ormond, her most important patient, the estate has two heirs: Howard and Fenton, Edsel's grandsons. But when Edsel informs Helen that he's decided to leave the property to Howard alone, on the condition that he first marries — and that the woman must be *her* — she realises her problems are only just beginning . . .